Journey to Gettysburg
One Family's Civil War

Robert J. Trout

ΠHP

Paths of History Publishers

Published by:
Paths of History Publishers, New York, New York
www.pathsofhistorypublishers.com

First Printing: April 2012

Cover Design: Deborah Schmitz Ross
Doll: Emma Crawford
Slingshot: Calvin Bricker
Hat: Robert J. Trout
Interior Design: Maureen Logan

Printed in the United States of America

Library of Congress Cataloging-in-Publication Data

Journey to Gettysburg: One Family's Civil War / Robert J. Trout

Summary: *Journey to Gettysburg: One Family's Civil War* tells the fictional story of a family living on a farm in Mercersburg, Pennsylvania when General J.E.B. Stuart and his Confederate Calvary came through town and changed their lives forever.

ISBN-13: 978-1469974996
Library of Congress Control Number 2012901649

1. JUVENILE FICTION / Historical Fiction / United States / Civil War Period (1861-1865). 2. JUVENILE FICTION / Boy Militia / Mercersburg Invincibles / Slingshot. 3. FICTION / Battle of Gettysburg / JEB Stuart / John Mosby / Gray Ghost. 4. FICTION / Historical Fiction / Family / Horses / Raids / Canals.

Also by Robert J. Trout

The Story of Red Eye:
The Miracle Horse of Gettysburg

Windrider

The Last Elf:
Quest for the Elfin Orb

Drumbeat: The Story of a
Civil War Drummer Boy

Contents

CHAPTER 1

The Mercersburg Invincibles

"**A**ttention! Forwaaarrrd, march!"

Thomas Jefferson Scott thoroughly enjoyed watching his friends and neighbors jump when he yelled at them – and he yelled a lot – while putting them through their drills. Mentally, he congratulated himself on coming up with the idea of forming a "Boy Militia" unit to defend Mercersburg against any and all enemies, especially any infernal Confederate Rebels that might threaten the town. The recent invasion of Maryland had panicked the residents of Mercersburg – not Tom Scott, of course – so something had to be done, and he decided he was the one to do it. While he couldn't take credit for school being closed during the harvest season, he had taken full advantage of it, taking every opportunity to bring the Invincibles together for more drilling. As he watched the twelve boys march back and forth carrying their ax or broom handles, his chest swelled with pride. Meanwhile, his head gave no thought of what boys armed with ax and broom handles could do to save the town if any infernal Confederate Rebels did come calling.

"Companeeeee! Halt! Private Boyd! Don't you got no notion of which foot's your left and which foot's your right?"

7

"Never had no need of knowin' which one was left or right before. Are they the same as my hands? I know them left from right."

"Course they's the same. Didn't your Ma ever tell you that? I swear. Now just march and think you're walkin' on your hands."

"If I walk on my hands, how'll I carry my broom handle?"

Tom took one step toward Billy with the idea of giving him a good thrashing, but suddenly remembered that he was the captain of the Mercersburg Invincibles and had to set a good example for his men. There were some sacrifices that an officer had to make, and not thrashing his men was one of them. He made a mental note to thrash Billy on a day the Invincibles didn't do any drilling.

"Captain Tom . . . I mean Captain Scott."

"Private Bricker. There ain't no talkin' in the ranks unless I talk to you first!"

"But I got chores. My Pa said if I was late one more time for chores, he'd make you do 'em for keepin' me too long."

"You told him you was with me?"

"Had to tell 'im somethin' and when I did, he said he'd make you do the chores I missed."

The very thought of chores of any kind gave Tom a headache. He steered clear of his own every chance he got, which was nearly every time he had to do them. He certainly didn't want to do anyone else's. Mr. Bricker was a stern man, rather large too. That, plus a rumbling in his stomach, reminding him that he hadn't eaten since noon, made Tom give in.

"Well, I guess we've done 'nough drillin' for today," he agreed at last. "Now don't forget to report here tomorrow after supper for more drillin'."

"Is it all right to call you Tom now," asked Jacob Smith, Tom's best friend, or rather, the only boy in Mercersburg who could put up with Tom's bullying for more than ten minutes without getting into a fight.

8

"Yeah, Jake. What's ailin' you?"

"I was wonderin' why we're doin' all this here drillin' and how we're goin' fight them infernal Confederate Rebels with ax and broom handles when they got guns?"

Tom stared at Jake long and hard. He noticed the other boys, except for Peter Bricker, racing across the field toward his house and gathering around with quizzical looks on their faces. He knew he couldn't admit that he really didn't know. Having heard his mother read a letter from her brother in the army, complaining about the constant drilling his officers put him through, Tom had thought that was all being in the army was – drilling and every once in awhile, fighting. He had asked old Mr. Bennett, a veteran of the War of 1812, how to drill so he could make the other boys do it. As far as the fighting was concerned, Tom never really believed that the Rebels would get any closer to Mercersburg than they had when they came into Maryland in September and fought along Antietam Creek near Sharpsburg. Of course, he couldn't tell the boys that or they would soon quit the Invincibles and he would have no one to order around.

"I'm . . ." Tom's head whirled, "I'm workin' on gettin' us weapons to fight with. We're only usin' the ax and broom handles 'til I get the . . ."

"You goin' to get us rifles like real soldiers have?" a bright-eyed Ben Rankin asked.

"Can't get no real soldier rifles 'cause the gover'ment uses them all, but I got somethin' just as good . . . almost."

Tom saw a cloud of doubt flash across Jake's face. He always had problems fooling Jake. Because they were afraid of him, the other boys very rarely questioned what Tom said. Jake was different. Nearly as big as Tom and once having fought Tom to a standstill, Jake was the only boy in or around Mercersburg who could question Tom and get away with it. Hoping to avoid having his bluff called, Tom added,

9

"Honest, I tell ya. I truly got somethin' almost as good."

"This better not be 'nother one of your lies, Tom," warned Jake, "'cause if it is . . ."

Tom leaned into Jake, trying hard to sound threatening, "You callin' me a liar, Jake Smith?"

Not backing down an inch, Jake glared into Tom's eyes, "Not yet, but I will if you don't have what you promise."

"I'll have it, and you'll eat your words."

"We'll see."

Walking home, Tom's mind scrambled about, searching frantically for something, anything, that he could deliver to the boys that would satisfy them, especially Jake. As he walked up the lane to his home, he grew more and more frustrated. Short of arming his "men" with bows and arrows, something they would never accept, his mind was a blank. Grumbling beneath his breath, he looked toward the barn and saw his father pitching hay down from the loft – one of the chores that Tom constantly dodged.

Jonathan Scott was a good man and a good father; Tom had to admit that. But he was ashamed of him still being here at home when so many other men from Mercersburg had joined the army. The word "coward," spoken in Tom's presence about his father by a few of the boys in town, had brought on several fights. Tom had won them all, but after each one he still wondered down deep inside if the boys were right. Was his father a coward? Other fathers were still at home, but they were older, while Jonathan Scott was still quite young. In the face of it all Tom had taken to talking less and less with his father; to finding reasons for staying away from home, even more than usual; and to stay away from boys, other than those who were in the Invincibles. Even a few of these he had caught lowering their heads and whispering when his father came near them in one of

Mercersburg's stores or in church. Tom was long past trying to ignore it or pretending that it didn't matter, so it ate away at him slowly, leaving behind a hollow feeling.

Going around to the front of the house so his father would not see him, Tom entered and made his way back to the kitchen, nearly falling over his sister, Ruth. Everyone who knew the Scotts thought that Ruth was a very strange child. Tom thought so too. Ruth had just turned five. She hadn't talked until she was four when she began to speak in clear, complete sentences, astonishing her family and unnerving friends and neighbors. However, she usually chose to say only one or two words at a time, just enough to be understood; or kept silent and to herself, playing with her doll, and the house cat, as well as other animals, including wild ones. Birds had been seen to perch on her shoulder and chirp into her ear. At a church picnic one day a year past, more than a dozen butterflies had landed on her, causing people to walk around her as if she had the typhoid fever. The ladies in Mercersburg decided that she had some kind of aura about her that others didn't have. It gave her peculiar "powers" they said, and they would not allow their children within fifty feet of her. The only person she seemed to relate to was her father. She followed him around during the day whenever she could, and snuggled up in his lap every night after supper and drifted off to sleep. Tom swore that on one such occasion, he heard her purring like a cat. In truth, she made him feel all goose-bumpy.

Rebecca Scott stood next to a table, mixing away at something in her favorite clay bowl that sat in front of her. She didn't look up from it as she scolded, "Thomas, you left your chores for your father again. He has enough work on this farm without trying to do yours as well. He needs your help and so do I."

Tom didn't answer. He had learned that it was best for him to

11

keep silent when he was in trouble. He knew his mother would soon go on to her own chores and leave him alone. He stepped back into the parlor, heading for his bedroom at the top of the stairs. He heard his mother call after him, "Please . . ." Before Mrs. Scott could say another word, Ruth stood up and followed him. Tom's eyes widened. It was almost as if she could read their minds. He looked at his mother who finished her request - "take your sister with you," and went back to her stirring.

Meals at the Scott household were eaten quickly and quietly. Only after everyone had finished was conversation permitted. Jonathan usually spoke first, recounting his day and any news he had heard from passing neighbors or from the town's citizens if he had gone into Mercersburg on some errand. Next, mother would relate any news she had heard, and read any letters the family had received. Every few days a letter from her brother brought news of the war. When she read them, Tom would look out the corner of his eye at his father, wondering how the letters made him feel. He always sat with his head down and eyes closed, as if he were listening very carefully to each word. Tom's turn came third, but he rarely said anything, adhering to his rule that the less his parents knew about where he had been and what he had been doing, the better. They didn't even know about the Invincibles yet. Ruth never said a word. She would just hold up a doll that had been sitting on her lap through the meal, hug it, and smile.

The next several days passed all too quickly, bringing Tom no closer to solving his "weapons" problem. During their drilling the boys pestered him about his promise, but a vicious glare usually caused them to change the subject. Jake didn't ask. Tom knew he was waiting until the day when the weapons were to appear. If they didn't, then Jake would have plenty to say. Tom didn't want to fight with Jake, but as the day drew closer without a solution, he resigned himself that he would have to. Then two days before he had to have his new weapons, a miracle occurred.

Sent on an errand to Mr. Shannon's Variety Store on the square in Mercersburg, Tom was near the Post Office when he felt a sharp pain in his leg and crumpled to the ground. Laughter from behind a clapboard fence told him where the rock that had struck him had come from. His leg really did hurt, so it was very easy to roll around on the ground and act like he had been badly injured. Keeping one eye on the fence while he rolled and moaned, Tom soon saw a board shift to one side and two young boys about six years old emerge. Tom recognized them from seeing them at various church services and picnics, though he didn't know their names. When they came close enough Tom jumped up and grabbed both of them by the neck.

"Which one of you done hit me with that rock?" Tom growled, trying to sound as fierce as possible.

"He did," the boys cried in unison, pointing fingers at each other.

Tom noticed that the boy on his right held an object that Tom had never seen before. "What's that?"

The boy dropped what he had been holding and sputtered, "What's what?"

"What you just dropped, and don't lie to me ag'in or I'll thrash you."

"It's a . . . a slingshot. Ain't you never seen a slingshot before?"

"No. Now, I'm goin' to let go of you both so you can show me how that there slingshot works, but if you try to run, I'll catch you and thrash you both."

"Can't catch us both if we run in different directions," offered the boy that had dropped the slingshot.

"No, but I can catch one today and the other tomorrow."

"Guess you could. All right, we won't run off. I'll show you

13

how it works."

For the next several minutes Tom sat completely absorbed in learning all there was to know about slingshots – though there wasn't much. The boys had certainly been practicing because they could hit what they aimed at six out of every ten shots, as they soon demonstrated. Tom tried a few times but couldn't hit anything. The boys laughed – once. A cuff on an ear of each of them ended that quickly. Even though he could not hit any targets the boys pointed out to him, Tom grew more and more excited. He had found the new weapon he could arm the Invincibles with. All he had to do was get more of them.

"Where'd you get this?" he asked, raising a clenched fist in front of the boy who had shot him.

"My pa made it for me. You have to have that springy stuff to make it work, and he has some."

"What is it?"

"He calls it rubber."

"Tain't never heard of the stuff. You ain't lyin' to me, are you?"

"I swear I ain't."

"Can you get me enough of this here rubber to make a dozen or so of these here slingshots, and show me how to make 'em?"

"Maybe we can get the rubber, but my pa made this one and I don't know how to."

"All right. You tell him you lost it and ask him for another one. Then you watch him make it. Watch him real close, 'cause if you can't tell me how to make one, I'll find you and thrash you good."

"But I didn't lose my slingshot. It's right here."

"I'm goin' to borrow it 'til you get me the rubber and find out how to make one. Then I'll give it back to you and each of you will have one."

The two boys talked to each other, thrilled with the idea of each having his own slingshot. At last one of them spoke up, "All right, but

I could get a whuppin."

"Why would you get a whuppin'?"

"My pa told me never to lie to him and I'm sure goin' to be lyin' if I tell him I lost my slingshot."

"Reckon you will, but I got to have this here slingshot for a couple of days. I promise I'll give it back as soon as you tell me how to make one and bring me the rubber. Now, how soon do you think your pa can make you another one?"

"Don't know. Maybe three or four days."

Tom didn't like that answer, but realized he couldn't push the boys too far or they would never do want he wanted. For once he would have to be patient – something he wasn't very good at. "Guess I can wait that long. We'll meet back here in three days. Agreed?"

Both boys nodded and started off. Tom stared down at the slingshot in his hands, studying it intensely. It didn't look too complicated. He hoped that he could make one and then remembered that he needed a dozen. The "Y" part looked like the partially carved fork of a tree branch. He decided to get a jump on the boys, find some tree branch forks, and start whittling.

The Mercersburg Invincibles stood at rigid attention in front of their captain. Tom felt the excitement that seemed almost to bubble out of each boy – except for Jake. His face revealed only doubt, with a hint of the anger that lay smoldering inside. Tom wasn't much for praying, thinking that it should only come at night when people could total up all the bad things they had done during the day and ask for forgiveness – he usually had a very long list, but he glanced skyward and muttered a little prayer anyway. He really didn't want to fight Jake. He liked Jake. Besides if he lost, he would no longer be captain of the Invincibles. Concentrating on the other boys and the thrill of expectation each had, he stepped forward, but before he could say a word Jake broke ranks. "You promised us new weapons. I don't see none."

Tom saw the other boys cast their eyes about, searching for the new weapons. Of course, there was nothing to see because Tom had the slingshot tucked into his pants behind his back and under his shirt. He reached back and pulled it out. Proudly, though with some fear, he held it up. Jake and the rest of the Invincibles stared at the strange looking device. Tom, noticing their faces sag, quickly reached down and picked up a pebble. Placing it in the slingshot he took aim at a tree trunk twenty feet away. He had been practicing with the slingshot at every opportunity and had improved immensely. He gulped, held his arm as steady as he could, and let fly. The loud "THWACK" echoing back at him told him he had hit what he had aimed at. Turning to face the Invincibles, he could see they were amazed, their eyes wide and their chins on their chests. Even Jake looked stunned.

"It's called a slingshot, and I'll be gettin' enough for all of us."

"Do it again!" yelled Billy.

Tom grabbed another pebble and plunked the tree trunk a second time. Now all the boys broke ranks and crowded around him. Cries of "Let me try!" filled the air. Tom noticed Jake slowly walking over to him. Pushing through the other boys, Tom handed Jake the slingshot with a, "Here, you try it." Jake took the slingshot and with Tom's help picked out a good pebble. He aimed at the trunk and fired. The pebble whizzed by, clipping a couple of leaves from a small tree behind the larger one. "You'll need a lot of practice. We all will. With these here slingshots we can shoot at the Rebels, and they won't even know where we are 'cause they don't make no noise and don't make no smoke."

Jake asked, sheepishly, "Can I try again?"

16

That night Tom's prayers included a very, very big "THANK YOU."

Tom had been waiting about a half- hour when the fence board creaked and the two young boys stepped out from behind it. One held a good-sized sack and the other a brand new slingshot.

"My pa made me another slingshot just like you said he would," the first boy began, "but he said if I lost this one, he'd never make me another one."

"Where is the rubber stuff?" asked Tom, ignoring what the boy said.

"Here in the sack. if my pa finds out I done took it he'll whup me good."

Grabbing the sack, Tom opened it and looked inside. Taking a quick count of its contents, he calculated that there were at least a dozen pieces of rubber, probably more, enough to make slingshots for all of the Invincibles.

"Can I have my slingshot now?" pleaded the boy.

"Not 'til you tell me how to make one," answered Tom, holding the slingshot high over his head where the boy could not reach it.

Half an hour later, after many questions and a careful study of both the new and the old slingshot, Tom felt he knew enough to make one of them by himself. He gave the slingshot to the boy who, with his friend, rapidly disappeared behind the fence. Tom dashed off down the street. He had three forks finished and had started a fourth. He could not hope to finish the rest before the next meeting of the Invincibles, but didn't really care.

Although they were disappointed at not having their own slingshots right away, the boys consoled themselves by taking turns shooting the ones that Tom had finished. Even Jake appeared to have fun testing his skill with the unusual weapon. Over the next several days, as Tom finished making the rest of the slingshots, he took time to practice as well, becoming a very good shot. The only problem he had was avoiding his chores, which meant avoiding his father and mother – not an easy thing to do, although he had become quite adept at it. Nevertheless, after sneaking in and out of the house – mornings and evenings, as necessary – and scrounging noontime meals from his friends, he finally gave up and stayed at home for three days, catching up on those chores that his father and mother had not had the time to do.

Meanwhile, the Invincibles practiced with their slingshots until each boy became an expert shot. Not surprisingly, although Tom would never admit it, Jake became the best shot. He could knock a particular leaf from a twig at ten paces, hit a fence post at twenty, and plunk a ten-inch tree trunk at thirty. The boys soon found that special care had to be taken with their weapons' ammunition. Not just any pebble would do. Searching stream beds for smooth stones occupied some drill time. Then Billy Boyd came up with a brilliant idea. He "borrowed" some of his father's round rifle ammunition. These lead pellets were a half-inch in diameter, flew straight and true, and hit with a wallop. Every boy's accuracy improved, and before long every Invincible carried a small leather pouch containing thirty or forty lead "pebbles," as well as a pocketful of smooth stream stones. Thus was born the great "missing ammunition" mystery that plagued a large number of hunters in and around Mercersburg at the end of September and the beginning of October, 1862.

News about the war continued to filter into Mercersburg through newspapers and letters from soldiers from the community who were now in the army. Letters from Tom's uncle revealed the Army of the Potomac's doings after Robert E. Lee's Army of Northern Virginia once again took up its defense of Virginia following the battle of

Antietam. Tom listened to his mother read the letters, but didn't think much about them until one afternoon while feeding the chickens; he ran out of feed and went to the barn for more. As he drew closer he heard his mother and father talking just inside the barn door.

"I don't care what the gossip is, Jonathan," Tom heard his mother say. "You and I know you are not a coward. You are staying here because I could not stand to lose both my brother and you in this war. He, you, and the children are all the family I have left in this world."

"But Rebecca," Jonathan argued, "you cannot know what might happen. Jeremiah has been in two battles and several skirmishes and has yet to be harmed."

"Every word you say is true, Jonathan, but it doesn't mean that he will escape the next one. Better you bear the whispers of those with loose tongues, than Thomas, Ruth, and I bear the loss of a father and husband."

"You do not see the downcast eyes when I go into town, or the people who wear mourning bands turning their backs to me as I pass by. I thought I could bear it all when I gave you my promise. Now . . . now I'm . . . I'm not sure I can."

"You would go back on your word?"

"No more than I would our wedding vows, but there may come a day when you must release me from my promise."

"And should I, how are we to survive?"

"Thomas is old enough to . . ."

"To run the farm. Yes, he and I could run it, but he shows no desire to. Indeed, he does all within his power to stay away from his chores. He is still a boy with wild adventure his only thought. No, Jonathan, he is not yet a man. You cannot lay the burden of this farm on his shoulders so you can go off and . . . and . . ."

"Very well. We will speak no more on this at present."

19

Tom nearly doubled over as if struck a blow to his stomach. He staggered back toward the chicken coop. His mother, not his father, bore the blame of keeping Jonathan Scott at home and out of the army, causing him to endure the shame of being labeled a coward. But even more than that, his mother didn't think her son man enough to help run the farm. At this thought, anger swelled within him. He nearly turned and ran back to the barn to argue that he was able. Then his mother's other words about how he shunned his chores and was yet a boy dreaming of adventures flashed into his mind. The truth of these bored deep inside him. He slumped down against a side of the chicken coop, tears welling in his eyes. At fourteen, he stood as tall as many of the men in Mercersburg. He could whip every boy his age, except maybe Jake on a bad day, and many older ones. He had never given a thought about what it was that made a man a man other than being grown up. How could doing his chores make him a man? Confused, he sat, head on knees, until his mother left the barn. His father followed soon after. Only then did he go and fill the feed bucket and return to feed the chickens, his mind still struggling with his mother's harsh, but all too true, words.

Although still bothered by what he had overheard, by the second week of October, Tom had managed to push it into the back of his mind by concentrating on the Invincibles. He paid another visit to Mr. Bennett and learned how to direct a firing drill. Now the boys loaded and fired their slingshots together, aiming and hitting a variety of targets, from trees to fences. Still, all the drilling and shooting began to become boring. Some of the boys questioned whether they were wasting their time drilling and target shooting when there didn't seem to be any chance of putting their abilities to good use. Not wanting to lose his position as captain of the town's only "Boy Militia," Tom came up with an idea for a practice "skirmish."

Tom divided the Invincibles into two groups with Jake, now a lieutenant, commanding one group and Tom the other, and armed each boy with small packets of cloth filled with chalk dust. Each side then took up positions about twenty paces apart. Going through the firing drill, they let loose several volleys at each other, a hit being scored when a boy was struck with a chalk packet. The lighter packets made hitting anything much more difficult than using a stone or lead ball. The entire exercise came to a halt when a packet hit Peter Bricker on the head, turning his hair and shoulders white when it burst. Both forces collapsed to the ground and spent the next several minutes rolling back and forth, taking turns laughing uproariously or gasping for air.

Jake hit upon the idea of entering Rankin's wood from opposite sides and skirmishing among the trees, again using chalk packets for ammunition. Tom's side won three "skirmishes" and Jake's won two. Standing in the lane after the last, the boys looked a sight with clothes, arms, and some heads giving evidence of the accuracy of their slingshots. The most successful attack had been the last of the day when Jake had concealed his "company" behind a raspberry thicket and waited for Tom's to pass by. Jake's boys delivered a volley that hit half of Tom's command, and the rest broke and ran. Tom was captured trying to rally his troops and had to surrender. Though somewhat embarrassed, Tom had to admit that Jake's plan had been a good one and that if any infernal Confederate Rebels ever showed their faces in Mercersburg, it just might work against them.

On Thursday, Tom had to cancel militia practice and accompany his father into town to purchase some needed items for the farm. Tom had often done so, but on those other occasions he hadn't paid much attention to the adults, always looking for his own friends. This day was different. Remembering what his father had said, Tom watched the men and women on the sidewalks and in the stores to see how they acted toward his father. It didn't take long to see the turning of heads; to hear the whispering; to experience the averting of the eyes that his father had spoken of. Once he had seen the truth of what his father had told his mother, Tom watched his father. All his life, Tom had seen his father walk among his neighbors with his head held high; his eyes looking ahead, straight and true; his bearing erect and proud. This day was different. With a face nearly pale, his back stooped over, and eyes cast downward, Jonathan Scott walked among his neighbors, an unwelcomed stranger. Not a single person talked to him or to Tom.

As they drove out along Oregon Street toward the farm, Tom asked, "Are you goin' to ask Ma to let you out of your promise?"

Jonathan Scott jerked his team of horses to a stop. "You been listening to your mother and me talk?"

"Couldn't help it. I was outside the barn and heard . . . I don't like the way the town folk look at you, Pa."

"Well, if you listened to what I told your mother, then you know I don't much care for it myself."

"Why don't you say somethin' back at those people?'

"Can't say something back when they don't say anything to you, now can you?"

"But you know what they're thinkin' 'bout you."

"Yes, I know, but until your mother releases me from my promise, I will have to endure it; and possibly worse."

"How can you make her change her mind?"

"Short of the Rebels marching down Franklin Street, I don't know, and I don't think that's going to happen anytime soon."

CHAPTER 2

Gray Dawn

om awoke to a gray sky and a rumbling like thunder in his stomach. Looking out of his bedroom window, he could see clouds heavy with rain in the distance. Though the road in front of the house was still dry, he knew that before the day was out, it would be wet and muddy. He had planned a drilling session for the Invincibles during the morning, not having been able to have one for a couple days. If only the rain held off until late in the afternoon or evening, he could still have it. Dressing, he hurried downstairs to breakfast, hoping to finish eating and leave the house before his father, already out doing the early morning chores, came in to eat.

At the bottom of the stairs through a wide open front door, Tom saw Ruth standing on the porch in her nightshirt, with two cooing morning doves settled at her feet. She faced south, staring into the distance. He called to her but received no answer, which didn't surprise him. Shaking his head, he approached her quietly, scaring away the doves, and looked out over her to see what she watched so intently. At that moment a large flight of grackles rose from the field across the road, dipping and swirling, as if one creature, before flying up and over the house. Ruth turned, looked up at him with her deep blue eyes, and pointed south. "Horses," she whispered. Tom lifted his head and strained to see what his sister saw. Seeing nothing but fields and woods, he muttered, "I don't see any horses." Again Ruth pointed and whispered, "Horses."

Another rumble from his stomach caused Tom to gently take his sister's hand and lead her back into the house. Believing that whatever Ruth "saw" must have been in her imagination, he lifted her from the floor, thinking how much she had grown and that he soon would not be able to pick her up so easily, and stepped into the kitchen. His mother, bending over an iron frying pan on the hearth, turned and smiled. She waved Tom toward a chair, and he slipped Ruth into it. He settled into the one next to it as his mother filled his plate with bacon, eggs, and a couple of griddlecakes. He ate ravenously. As he stuffed the last of a griddlecake into his mouth, his father opened the kitchen door. Tom avoided looking at him, thinking that he could still slip away if his father started eating, but it was not to be.

"Ah ... Thomas," his father sighed. "I'm happy I caught you before you left this morning. It looks like rain will be coming sometime today. I'd like to do some threshing in the barn this afternoon. I could sure use some help."

Taking the hint and figuring that he could not drill in the rain anyway, he answered, "I promised to meet some of the boys this morning, but I'll come back and help you."

"Good, we'll start sometime after lunch."

That settled, though not entirely to his satisfaction, Tom excused himself, grabbed his coat as he had felt a chill in the air when he brought in Ruth from the porch, and left through the kitchen door. He first ran to the barn to retrieve his slingshot and ammunition from under a loose board, his special hiding place, and started across the field toward the creek. For whatever reason, he could not get what Ruth had said out of his mind. She rarely said anything, but when she did he had learned to pay attention to it – strange as it might be. He took a quick glance to the south, saw nothing as before, shrugged, and took off at a steady pace across the field, trying to run between the corn stalks and not through them.

Jake, Billy, and Ben were already gathered around the great tree down by Johnston Run. Each carried an ax or broom handle that the Invincibles still used for drilling. But each also had his slingshot tucked into his pants, with his ammunition pouch swinging from his belt. Tom nodded at Jake who nodded back.

"Hope we can get this drillin' done fast so we can get in some target shootin'," Billy offered.

"Me, too," agreed Ben. "I'm gettin' to be a pretty good shot."

"So, you're finally starting to hit the side of your barn," teased Jake.

"Ahhhh, come on, Jake. You know I've gotten better."

"Hey! Here come some of the other fellers," interrupted Tom.

Half the morning had passed before the company assembled. *Chores!* thought Tom before barking, "Fall in!"

"Hope he doesn't mean into the creek," muttered Peter.

Laughter broke from several of the boys who heard Peter, causing Tom to yell, "Attention!" He would have yelled it anyway, but Peter had supplied him with an added reason. Tom soon noticed that Johnny Myers, the smallest and youngest boy in the Invincibles, had not yet arrived. "Company Halt!" called Tom. "Attention! Any of you seen Johnny, I mean Private Myers, today?"

A shaking of heads convinced Tom that no one had, and he concluded that Johnny was probably still doing his farm work. Being somewhat small, it took him longer than the other boys. Shrugging his shoulders, Tom went back to drilling his "men." After a good half-hour, he ordered, "Halt!" and added a "Prepare for target practice!"

For the next thirty minutes, the sound of stones plunking off tree trunks filled the air. Each boy shot individually until Tom brought the company together to practice volley fire. After that, contests of accuracy at different distances helped sharpen firing skills. Tom had just bested Jake with an amazing shot at forty paces when Johnny came dashing up the path next to the creek. Dropping to his knees from his effort, he fought to catch his breath, finally managing to blurt out between gulps of air, "Soldiers . . . cavalry soldiers . . . ridin' . . . into . . . town. Gotta come . . . and see."

"Gee!" exclaimed Billy. "I tain't never seen no cavalry before. How many are there?"

"I . . . I . . . don't . . . rightly know. I saw about a dozen . . . I guess."

"Cavalry in Mercersburg?" questioned Tom. "Why would cavalry come through our town?" Then a tingling sensation formed at the base of his spine that migrated upward and caused the hairs at the base of his neck to stand on end. Ruth had known they were coming. Somehow she had known. He shuddered with the thought.

"Maybe they're goin' to join the army," suggested Jake.

"Let's go see them!" pleaded Ben.

"Yeah, let's go. What do you say, Captain?"

Jake's question brought Tom back from where he had been, and didn't really want to be. Willing to do anything that would help remove the eerie feeling that engulfed him, he answered with, "Company dismissed!" Caught up in the excitement, the boys bolted for the path along the creek and raced toward town. At first Tom lagged behind, but his size and strength soon catapulted him into the lead, the rest of the Invincibles strung out behind him. Just beyond Mr. Martin's yard, Tom left the path and ran down a narrow alley to Oregon Street. Crossing it, he led the pack of chattering boys along the back yards of the houses that stretched along the east side of Fayette Street. A shot rang out and with it all thoughts of his sister vanished from Tom's mind. He and the others dived for cover into some bushes behind the home of Mr. Shaffer, who sometimes bought eggs from the Scotts.

"What was that?" puzzled Billy.

"Sounded like a shot to me," answered Jake.

"Do you think they was shootin' at us?"

"Why would they shoot at us, and who's 'they'?"

"Hey! Look there. Tain't that Mr. Shaffer with a gun?" asked Tom, pointing to the yard in back of one of the houses along the street.

Suddenly, four mounted men dressed in blue overcoats came riding along the back of the house from the direction of Seminary Street, their carbines nestled in the crooks of their arms. They looked very angry, and riding up to Mr. Shaffer, they surrounded him. One of the men yelled, "Did y'all fire that there shot?"

Tom looked at Jake, and Jake looked at Tom. At the same time they said, "Them's infernal Confederate Rebels!" before turning their attention back to Mr. Shaffer and the mounted men.

"I was just trying to shoot a chicken for my supper, and what business is it of yours, may I ask? I can shoot chickens in my own back yard if I have a mind to," responded Mr. Shaffer indignantly.

"A chicken!" another of the mounted soldiers mocked. "I think you fired on the great Palmetto flag of South Carolina and the gallant men who serve under her. Besides, I don't see no chickens."

"Of course you don't see any chickens. I missed and you scared them off." After a thoughtful pause, Mr. Shaffer added, "Did you say South Carolina?"

"I did indeed sir. We are of Colonel Butler's Second South Carolina Cavalry under the command of Maj. Gen. Jeb Stuart."

27

"Impossible! There are no Rebels north of the Potomac River."

"You hear that boys. We must've took the wrong road back at Opequon Creek in Ol' Virginny."

As the four men broke into laughter, Tom gawked at them. Real Rebels. Here in Mercersburg. He swallowed hard. Turning to look at Jake, he saw all of the boys staring at him. *Why are they all looking at me?* He wondered. Slowly he began to understand. He had formed the Mercersburg Invincibles to fight any infernal Confederate Rebels who dared come into Mercersburg. Now those infernal Confederate Rebels were here, right in front of him. By a remarkable twist of fate, his company of Invincibles was right there with him – and they were armed with the weapons he had made for them. Tom's head swiveled between the Rebels and the Invincibles several times before Jake whispered, "Well, Captain Scott, what are your orders?"

Before Tom could answer, everyone's attention refocused on Mr. Shaffer and the Rebels. The Rebel who seemed to be in charge of the others ordered, "Y'all have to come with us. Colonel Butler'll have to decide what's to be done with you. Maybe even General Stuart hisself will decide. Could be ol' Libby Prison for you."

"I certainly will not go with you anywhere. I have . . ." argued Mr. Shaffer, but his next words caught in his throat as the black mouths of four carbines were aimed at him. Reluctantly he handed over his own rifle and fell in behind two of the cavalrymen's horses, his face turning paler by the second.

Jake nudged Tom almost growling at him, "What're we going to do? We can't just let them take Mr. Shaffer without doin' somethin'."

Jake's words spurred Tom to action. Stretching his neck to look over Jake at the rest of the Invincibles he whispered, "Prepare to fire in volley. Use the rifle ammunition."

Seconds ticked by. Their training had prepared the Invincibles

28

for just such a moment. Their slingshots loaded they waited until Tom ordered, "Stand!"

As one, the Invincibles rose up from behind the bushes. Tom took the scene in at a glance. Two of the cavalrymen were several yards off, walking their horses back toward Seminary Street. Mr. Shaffer, his head down, followed. A third soldier also had turned his horse in the direction of the others, but the fourth still sat his horse a few paces away, staring into the back yards of the houses. Just as he began to rein his horse around his eyes fell on the boys. At that moment Tom barked, "Ready! Aim! Fire!"

Thirteen lead bullets twanged from the leather pockets of the Invincibles' slingshots, each one of them finding their mark somewhere on the head and body of the Rebel cavalryman. With a yelp he careened from the saddle and fell to the ground. Hearing his friend's cry, the soldier in front of him swung around to see what had happened. Tom and the Invincibles greeted him with a volley that nearly knocked him from his horse. Meanwhile the first soldier had risen from the ground, rubbing several places on his head and chest. The Invincibles launched another volley at him, forcing him to drop to the ground a second time.

Tom had just ordered the Invincibles to reload when he saw a third cavalryman, one of the two that had ridden off with Mr. Shaffer, riding directly toward him behind the bushes. Being on that end of the Invincibles' line, Tom managed to get off one shot from his slingshot that struck the man in the chest but failed to stop him. Several of the other boys now saw the man and fired wildly at him, none striking their target. As horse and rider thundered down on them, the Invincibles broke and ran in those directions that led away from the Rebels. Tom, his legs rooted in place, watched them run. The two soldiers on the other side of the bushes, both now firmly mounted once again, chased after the fleeing boys.

"Drop that there . . .," Tom's captor yelled, not really knowing what to call the strange device in Tom's hand.

"Slingshot. It's a slingshot," Tom finished the soldier's sentence, as he dropped his weapon to the ground.

"You too, young feller."

Tom twisted his head around to see Jake standing behind him. "Couldn't let you get captured all by yourself. Besides, I missed him with my first shot and was tryin' to get another one off. Weren't fast enough."

The two other cavalrymen returned with three other Invincibles, including Billy and Ben. One of the soldiers asked, "What're we goin' to do with 'em? They's just younguns."

"I 'spect we'll hav'ta take 'em to Colonel Butler along with that other feller," replied Tom and Jake's soldier.

After all the slingshots had been picked up and all the ammunition taken from the boys, including the emptying of stones from pockets, the little party slowly marched after the first soldier and Mr. Shaffer. Tom, Jake, and the other boys stole furtive glances at the Rebels that crowded close to them on three sides. They looked scruffy; their clothes dirty; their equipment worn; and their horses tired. Still, Tom had to admit that they did not look like the kind of men who would run at the first shot, as he had often been told the Rebels did. Their lean, weather-beaten faces had a hard look about them. These men were real soldiers, and the fact that they occupied Mercersburg meant that they had ridden around or through the Union army. They were bold and daring men. Tom's insides churned. *What would such men do to him and the other boys?*

Reaching Seminary Street, the little column stopped to allow a small group of soldiers to ride by in the direction of the theological seminary. One of them called out, "Colonel Butler has given orders to secure the town. No one in and no one out without his permission. We're to picket this here road and send a squad out to bring in horses. Too bad you boys got to watch pris'ners. Looks like you got a mean bunch there." Amidst several loud guffaws, the group passed on. Grumbling to themselves, the four cavalrymen led their captives west toward the town square. All along Seminary Street people crowded onto their porches or stood outside their doors, too curious to go back inside their homes and too frightened to venture any further from them. Tom tried to see ahead but could glimpse only what looked like many mounted men riding back and forth or standing along the sides of the street.

Mercersburg's square teemed with activity. A long column of men, four across, rode up Franklin Street toward Johnston Run. Many of the invaders wore gray, not blue, sending shivers up and down Tom's spine. A loud clattering of horses' hooves and jingling harnesses alerted Tom that something terrible approached. Ordered to "Halt!" just outside McKinstry's store, Tom gaped wide-eyed as two huge cannon rolled onto the square. They appeared monstrous, their wide muzzles seeming to leer at him like two pitch black eyes. He turned away to see the door to Mr. Brewer's store across Franklin Street standing wide open. Empty-handed soldiers entered through it while others, their arms full, came out. Most carried at least one pair of boots or shoes and other items that Tom could not identify from where he stood. Tom looked at Mr. Shannon's store and saw the same thing. If this kept up, nothing would be left in any store in town. Through the crowd of men and horses he could see someone pumping water into the trough in front of Colonel Murphy's hotel across the square. Soldiers were filling their canteens while their horses drank from the trough. Tom wondered if they might drink the well dry. A shout drew his attention back to his own predicament.

"Private Griggs!" barked a man who approached the group on foot, leading a bay horse. "What have you brought me?"

One of the soldiers saluted and answered, "Cap'in Gary. This here man fired this here rifle at us and . . ."

"Private you look like you fell off your horse. Were you struck?"

"Yes and no, Cap'in."

"Well, speak up, Private. What happened to you? Did this man shoot at you?"

"To tell you the truth, Cap'in, he says he was shootin' at a chicken fer his supper. We didn't 'xactly see him shoot in our direction."

"Then why do you look like you were knocked to the ground? I can't be persuaded that as fine a horseman as you simply fell off his mount."

"We was ambushed, Cap'in, by these here boys shootin' these here contraptions called slingshots. They fired these here lead bullets at us and knocked me off my horse."

For a time, Captain Gary studied the slingshot and the lead ammunition from one of the pouches that Private Griggs handed to him. Having quickly figured out how the slingshot worked, the captain loaded it with a lead bullet and fired it at a nearby tree trunk. He missed, striking the side of a house instead. "Lucky for you they didn't hit you in a vital spot."

"They did hit me a couple of times in the head and face, Cap'in."

"Like I said, lucky for you they didn't hit you in a vital spot."

After his fellow soldiers stopped chuckling, Private Griggs asked, "Yes, Cap'in, but what y'all want me to do with 'em?"

"I suspect that Colonel Butler will want to question them, so keep them here under guard for the time being. I'll talk to the colonel as soon as I can. Don't let any of your men wander off into the stores.

You're charged with guarding these prisoners. If they escape, you'll answer for it."

"Yes, Cap'in."

Mr. Shaffer, Tom, and the other boys walked over to the side of McKinstry's store and sat down, leaning their backs against the wall. Three of the soldiers dismounted, handing the reins of their horses to the fourth, and with their carbines took positions facing their prisoners.

Jake leaned over and muttered softly, "Whatd'ya think they're goin' to do to us, Tom? Think they'll take us to that there Liddy Prison?"

"I think it was Libby Prison, and I don't know what they'll do with us, or to us. My ma was worried about Uncle Jeremiah off fightin' in the war and now here come the war right to our doorstep and me in the middle of it."

"Yeah. Are you scared?"

"Sure I'm scared, but I ain't goin' to let them Rebels know it if I can help it. Hey, the Invincibles sure gave them a fight. Didn't we?"

"Sure did. Wonder what happened to the rest of the boys? Hope they got away."

As he talked, Tom watched as more and more Rebels poured though Mercersburg. He also saw many riderless horses being led by the gray cavalrymen. Two of the gray-clad men broke from the long column and trotted over toward where he sat. Each soldier had four horses trailing behind him. The first one reined to a stop and called out to Private Griggs, "Too bad George. Y'all missed all the fun. While y'all was roundin' up pris'ners, we was roundin' up all these here horses. Got this one I'm ridin' at a farm west of town. Just in time too. My horse was 'bout wore out. Ain't he a beauty?"

"Looks fine, I guess," mumbled Private Griggs somewhat

dejectedly.

"Say, George. Did y'all get into some kinda scrap? Y'all look a mite beat up."

"He got knocked from his horse by these here boys firin' these here slingshot contraptions," volunteered one of Tom's guards.

Private Griggs threw the man a dirty look and tried to change the subject. "Frank," he pleaded to the mounted man, "my horse is done in too. Think y'all could swap one of those y'all got there fer mine?"

"Sorry. Y'all will haveta ask Colonel Butler. We was told we could swap ours, but he didn't say nothin' about lettin' others do it."

"All right, Frank. I can't figure out how I always get the rotten details. Got to guard pris'ners. Can't take any horses. Can't go into any stores. And it'll probably rain before the day is out and I ain't got no poncho."

"Y'all jus' don't live right, George."

"Live jus' like y'all do."

"Can't be. If y'all did, y'all wouldn't be guardin' them there pris'ners. Y'all would be ridin' a new horse and visitin' in all these here stores, and y'all would have a poncho." And with howling laughs the two soldiers rode away, leaving Private George turning redder by the second. He whirled on his companions and growled, "Don't nonna y'all say nothin' or . . ." Then he turned toward Tom and the Invincibles, adding, "and don't nonna y'all try anything. I'd hate to have to explain to the cap'in why I hadda shoot ya," and walked back to his place on guard.

"Do you really think he'd shoot us?" asked Ben quietly, his voice quivering and his face filled with fright.

"Naw," answered Tom, trying to sound as reassuring as he could. "He's just sore. He can't hurt us if we don't do nothin' 'cause he's got to take us to that colonel feller."

34

"I pray that's so."

"I never done much prayin'," admitted Billy. "Guess I better start right now."

At that instant, another group of soldiers came around the corner leading the rest of the Invincibles, with Peter Bricker in the lead. Herded over to the wall, the boys squatted down next to their friends. "Thought you got away," muttered Tom to Peter.

"We did, for awhile," responded Peter quietly, "but ran into another bunch of them there fellers."

"Well, what happened?"

"After we left you and Jake . . . I'm really sorry 'bout that, Tom. We just saw that there cavalry feller come ridin' down on you and I jus' got all scared and . . ."

"That's okay, Pete. Jake and I were scared out of our wits too. So scared our feet couldn't move. If they could've, we would've been with you. Now how'd you get caught?"

"Like I said, we ran, but some of us ain't as quick as others, so they got caught. Rest of us met up behind Mr. Martin's fence and tried to catch our breaths. I wanted to come back for you and Jake and the others, but before we could make a plan we heard more horses. We thought they was lookin' for us, so we decided to keep quiet and maybe they would ride right by."

"That's what all of us wanted to do," interrupted Johnny Myers, "but Pete says we were Invincibles and we're supposed to protect the town and that we should fight. So we loaded up and waited until them soldiers was right in front of us. Pete said we should aim for their horses 'cause there weren't many of us and the horses were bigger targets. He said he once saw a horse stung by a hornet go crazy, buckin' all over the place. So we stood up and fired at the horses of the first three riders. I think there was ten all t'gether."

"That was smart thinking, Pete," congratulated Tom. "I'm goin' have to make you a sergeant. Did ya hit 'em?"

"Hit all three," continued Pete, "and I tell ya, Tom, I ain't never seen such abuckin' and ajumpin' and asnortin' and aswearin' in all my life. Them first three horses banged into all the others and before you knew it, all them there Rebel fellers were flyin' through the air with their hats and rifles and other stuff goin' every which away. Hey! Did you say I was a sergeant?"

"Yeah. Yeah. Now go on. How'd you get captured?"

"Well, we let loose a couple a more volleys. Couldn't hardly miss. That jus' made them there horses even more madder than they was already. They started runnin' off in every direction with the Rebels runnin' after them. We started hootin' and hollerin' and I guess we should've been watchin' out, 'cause before we knows it six more of them Rebel fellers come ridin' down the street. Before I saw them, they sent two down the alley next to Martin's and cut us off from the creek. The other four rode right up to the fence and pointed their rifles at us. Tom, I was so sacred I swear my knees was knockin'. I thought they was goin' to shoot us, but they jus' said we should climb over the fence and give 'em our shootin' contraptions. So we did, and here we are."

Tom could not believe his ears. Of all the boys in the Invincibles, Peter Bricker was the last one he had thought would put up such a fight, except for Johnny Myers, him being so small. But the two of them and the others had put up a fight. A better one than Jake and he had. Tom smiled. His invincibles had given a good account of themselves. While the rest of the townspeople had been caught completely unprepared for the enemy, the Invincibles had given the enemy battle and for a short time defeated them. But in the end, slingshots in the hands of thirteen boys could not match rifles in the

36

hands of hundreds of grown men – and hardened soldiers to boot. Again the question loomed before him in his mind - *What would the Rebels do to him and the rest?*

As Tom and the Invincibles awaited their fate, the Rebels brought other prisoners to join them and Mr. Shaffer. Tom recognized Mr. Blair, publisher of the *Good Intent*, and Mr. Rupley, a town official. Some of the other men looked familiar, but neither Tom nor any of the other boys knew their names. The men walked over to Mr. Shaffer and began talking in low voices. Tom heard them say that they would be taken along with the Rebels. Maybe that was what would happen to the Invincibles as well.

If possible, the town square looked even more crowded than before. A number of the town's residents stood around the outskirts of the square and gawked at the Rebel horde. The soldiers didn't seem to bother them, being more concerned with the horses they had confiscated or what they could find in the stores. Several people attempted to talk to the prisoners, but Private Griggs would not allow it. One of Tom's neighbors yelled, "Tom! Tom! Why are you and the other boys being held?" One of the guards quickly pushed him away, but not before he yelled, "I'll tell your parents."

A wave of goose bumps swept over Tom. His parents! He had not even thought about them during this whole time. And what of the other boys' parents? When they all found out that the Invincibles had been his idea – that might be worse than the Rebels hauling him off as a prisoner. Then, a picture of his mother standing outside Brewer's store, waving good-bye to him and crying, flashed before him. Next she was on her knees in front of Private Griggs, begging him not to take her little boy away from her. The other boys' mothers stood around her, weeping into handkerchiefs that dripped water on the ground. He could hear his father and some of the other fathers calling, "Take us instead! Leave our boys with their mothers!" Little Ruth sat on the ground next to her mother and pointed at the Rebels saying, "Horses." Tom closed his eyes and shook his head to clear it. Finally, the only image that remained was of his sister, now standing on their front porch, pointing south, and saying, "Horses." How had she known?

"Private Griggs!"

Captain Gary's yell jerked Tom from his daydream.

"Colonel Butler wants you to bring the prisoners to him. Hurry along with them. The colonel's in a foul mood."

With about a half-a-dozen soldiers surrounding them, the prisoners tramped across Seminary Street and passed one of the giant cannon. Sitting on a horse next to it was a very young looking soldier with blond hair and blue eyes. Tom thought the soldier didn't look old enough to really be a soldier. He heard one of the men sitting on a horse next to him say, "Major Pelham. Captain Breathed sends his compliments and says that his guns will be along in a few minutes. He wishes to know where you want them." Moving on, Tom did not hear the answer, but he stared back over his shoulder, marveling how so young a soldier, who looked about the same age as Tom himself, could possibly be an officer. A minute later the prisoners halted in front of another very young looking man with three stars on the collar of his jacket. Private Griggs made himself as straight as a fence post, saluted, and said, "Colonel Butler. Private Griggs reportin' with the pris'ners as ordered."

"Private, Captain Gary informed me that you were attacked by a number of boys armed with what I believe he called slingshots. Is that true?"

Private Griggs shuffled a little from one foot to the other and cleared his throat before answering. "Well, yes Colonel. About a dozen of 'em popped out from behind some brush and shot at us with what they said was slingshots."

"And do you have one of these . . . slingshots with you?"

"Yes, sir."

"May I see it?"

"Yes, sir."

Private Griggs handed a slingshot to Colonel Butler along with a couple of lead bullets. Tom watched as Colonel Butler examined it as Captain Gary had. After a couple of minutes, the colonel fitted a lead bullet into the leather patch, pulled back, aiming at a tree close by, and fired. More accurate than the captain, Colonel Butler grinned as his shot thwacked into the tree's trunk. "Captain Gary tells me that you were knocked off your horse, Private. That true?"

Gulping hard, Private Griggs answered, "Yes, sir, but they took me by surprise, sir. I . . ."

"It's all right, Private. I can see how a dozen of these lead pellets hitting a man with such force might easily cause him to vacate his saddle. An ingenious device, this slingshot." Turning to the boys clumped in a tight group, Colonel Butler asked, "I suppose you have a leader?"

Now it was Tom's turn to gulp hard, which he did several times before finding his voice. "I'm the captain of the Mercersburg Invincibles," he managed to say at last.

"The Mercersburg Invincibles! Oh, yes. I see. You're the town's militia."

Jake now stepped forward, "We are, and we are sworn to protect it from infernal Confederate Rebels."

"INFERNAL CONFEDERATE REBELS! Wait until General Stuart hears this! Private, you will hold these 'Invincibles' and the rest of your prisoners, who, I might say, do not look so nearly as dangerous, until such time as General Stuart can question them. Captain . . . I am sorry, I don't know your name."

Tom gulped some more and then answered in as firm a voice as he could muster, "Captain Scott. Captain Thomas Jefferson Scott."

"Well, Captain Thomas Jefferson Scott, Major General J. E. B. Stuart will decide what is to be done with you, and I can tell you that being named after a great Virginian will not gain for you and your Invincibles an ounce of mercy. You have fired from ambush on soldiers of the Confederate States, something that General Stuart does not abide. I greatly fear that Libby Prison, or worse, awaits you and your men."

Tom blanched white, as did all the Invincibles. In their moment of fear they did not see the wink that Colonel Butler threw to Captain Gary. Had they, the next hour would not have been the longest of their lives.

CHAPTER 3

Jeb Stuart

Shuffled off to one side by the guards, the prisoners either sat down or stood around, muttering and mumbling about their situation. Tom found it difficult to breathe and so said nothing. The rest of the Invincibles talked little, each boy's thoughts churning around in his mind and conjuring up all kinds of terrors, especially about the "worse" that Colonel Butler had mentioned. Fear of General Stuart and what he might do to them grew and grew. Johnny Myers started to cry, and several of the other boys looked like they would soon join him. Jake elbowed Tom in the ribs and pointed to an officer riding up to Colonel Butler. "You think that might be General Stuart?" Jake whispered. "He don't look so mean." Tom strained to hear what passed between the two men.

"Good day, Lieutenant Price. I suspect that General Stuart cannot be far behind you."

"Colonel Butler. The general sends his compliments and wishes to know if the town has been made secure."

"You may tell the general that all the roads are picketed to a half mile out, and all the town's streets are guarded. Except for some minor resistance, on which I shall report to him myself, all has been quiet. It does not appear that the town had any warning of our approach and the residents were taken completely by surprise. I don't believe they will give us any trouble."

"The general will be pleased to hear that. I see that your men have been shopping in the stores."

"Yes, there are a number of items the men have in short supply that these stores have in abundance."

"The general wanted me to repeat his orders that the citizens' homes are not be touched and that any goods taken from merchants be paid for."

"No homes will be violated and all goods will be paid for in good Confederate script."

"General Stuart also wanted me to inquire about the arrest of any public figures that could be used to exchange for our officials taken by the enemy in Virginia."

"We have arrested several. They are over there."

"Colonel, your men appear to be guarding those boys. Are they?"

"It is a long story, Lieutenant. One that I will share with the general."

"Very well. I shall be interested to hear it myself."

Tom and Jake watched as Lieutenant Price saluted and cantered off. Colonel Butler glanced in their direction, threw them a stern look, and rode into the middle of the street. Minutes later the two boys saw a bearded officer wearing a feather in a wide-brimmed hat, accompanied by several other officers, stop alongside Colonel Butler, who saluted. Neither of the boys could hear what was being said, but suddenly Colonel Butler swiveled around in his saddle and pointed directly at them. Tom and Jake tried to make themselves as small and inconspicuous as possible, but without something to hide behind, their efforts proved useless. They saw the bearded officer, whom they now were sure was General Stuart himself, nod his head several times. He had been smiling when he first greeted Colonel Butler. Now his face changed as his brow furrowed and his jaw set. "Whatever the colonel's tellin' him can't be good," Jake observed.

"And you know he's tellin' 'im 'bout us. Jake, I'm sorry I got you and the others into this. I never thought . . ."

"Neither did I. How could you know the Rebels were goin' to come right through Mercersburg? Besides, I was the one who made you shoot at that Private Griggs feller."

"Jake, I'm more scared than I ever was in my whole life."

"Me too."

"But we can't let the other boys know it. When General Stuart questions us, I'll take the blame and maybe he'll let the rest of you go."

"You feelin' all right, Tom. You ain't never took the blame for nothing."

"Well, those other times were different. Besides I'm captain of the Invincibles, so it's my duty.

"And I'm the lieutenant, so I'm goin' to tell him I'm with you."

"Thanks, Jake. I was sure hopin' you'd be with me."

Looking back at the group of officers, the boys watched General Stuart and his staff ride off. They stopped for a moment outside Brewer's store, talked with some of the soldiers, and looked at the things they carried. Then they trotted off, going north on Franklin Street and disappearing into the mass of mounted men.

Having been distracted by watching General Stuart, Tom did not see Colonel Butler ride up to them. "Captain Scott," he called out. "I have told General Stuart about you and your Invincibles. He was greatly interested in you and what you did. I will be sending you and your men and the other prisoners to see him shortly. If I were

43

you, I should be sure to tell him the truth. Along with ambushers, General Stuart cannot tolerate liars. It would be best for you and your men if you were not both. One of the two will be bad enough."

When it came, the march up Franklin Street under guard seemed to take forever. Ringed by mounted soldiers, the Invincibles and the other prisoners walked quietly along. Many people lined the street, stretching their necks to see whom the Rebels had taken. Some called out names. Tom heard. "There's Daniel Shaffer." "They've got Cornelius Louderbaugh." "Isn't that William Raby and Mr. Rupley?" Tom even heard his name and some of the boys' names called out. One shout stabbed deep into him. "That's my boy! Johnny! Johnny Myers! Oh, what are they going to do to him?" He heard Johnny cry out, "Ma! Ma!" and try to run to her but the soldiers stopped him. Tom saw Johnny's mother reach out to him, but one of the cavalrymen's horses blocked her from reaching her son. Knowing that he could do nothing to help, Tom looked away, his eyes filling with moisture. He hardly ever cried. Boys were supposed to be tough, but he had never felt like he felt now, even when Patch, his dog, had died a few years back. No, this was different. Somehow he had to get General Stuart to let the Invincibles go.

The captives trudged over the arched stone bridge that spanned Johnston Run. The guards directed everyone into a large yard to the left of the road. Horses, their reins held by soldiers, stood about the yard. Tom noticed General Stuart and several of his officers standing on a porch talking to a lady he recognized as Mrs. Steiger. Tom had heard that her two boys were sick with the measles. Before long a few officers entered the house and quickly emerged, carrying chairs and a table that they placed on the porch. The men sat down around the table, and Mrs. Steiger disappeared into the house. Tom smiled. Even infernal Confederate Rebels were afraid of measles.

Private Griggs barked, "Halt! You pris'ners sit yourselves down right where you're standin'. Gen'ral Stuart wants ta talk ta y'all."

Suddenly a man galloped over the bridge, reining his horse to a stop in front of the house. He leaped off the animal's back and ran along the side of the house to the porch, carrying what looked like a small canvas bag. Sitting only a few feet away, Tom heard every word.

"Captain Blackford," called General Stuart. "I wondered where you had ridden off to. What have you there?"

"A map, General. A map of this county, and you will not believe the danger I encountered securing it for your use."

"Danger? In this peaceful place. Don't keep all of us in suspense a moment longer. Tell us of your adventure."

"Our scout, Logan, who once worked for a Mr. Herman Hause here in Mercersburg before the war, informed me that a map of the county hung on a wall in the Hause home. Knowing our need for such a map, I determined to requisition it. Upon reaching the house, I knocked on the door and was greeted by several ladies, all of whom denied quite vigorously the existence of such a map. I insisted that I had it on good authority that the map did exist and that they must be attempting to mislead me."

"Why Captain Blackford," teased General Stuart, "you have always had the most cordial associations with the ladies we have met. Could it be that you appeal only to ladies of the Southern persuasion?"

"I assure you, General, I appealed to these ladies most earnestly but to no avail. In the end I fear that I had no choice but to break one of your orders and force my way into the house under a barrage of oaths that would have made the least gentlemanly of your soldiers blush. I found the map precisely where Logan said it would be, cut it from its rollers, and stuffed it in my haversack. As I left, I was again subjected to the most unladylike language and in truth believe that I was fortunate to escape without serious injury."

Stuart and the other officers burst out into hearty laughter, all turning rose-red from their exertions. When at last they gained their breaths, General Stuart spoke, "I suppose I should take a look at this map that almost cost me my engineer officer, and see if it was worth his gallant sacrifice." For several minutes General Stuart, Captain Blackford, and the other officers studied the map. They appeared to be plotting out a route, but Tom could not be sure because they kept their voices quiet, not wanting anyone else to hear what they planned.

Soon a soldier came running from the road and said something to General Stuart. The soldier left and almost immediately returned with a man that Tom recognized - Mr. George W. Wolfe, Mercersburg's constable. He wasted no time and addressed General Stuart without the customary introductions. "Your men informed me that you are General Stuart and that you have given orders to confiscate any and all horses belonging to the citizens in and around Mercersburg. Your men have stolen seven of my horses and have left me with two worthless, worn out animals. I ask that you stop such thievery and return all the horses your men have taken thus far."

Tom saw General Stuart's face grow very serious. He stepped forward and looked down at Mr. Wolfe from the edge of the porch. "Sir, believe me that I deeply regret having to take horses from you and the other citizens of this beautiful state, but surely you know there is a war being fought that each side is attempting to win. Your soldiers have removed countless animals and possessions from my state of Virginia. Our army is in desperate need of horses and mules. I have no choice but to gather all that I can for my cause. Neither your horses nor any others will be returned. They are now the property of the Confederate States."

During General Stuart's reply, Tom saw Mr. Wolfe glance at the group of prisoners, his eyes widening as he realized the danger in which he had placed himself. Having heard that the Rebels were arresting any town official that might be exchanged for one of theirs, Tom knew that if the Rebels found out that Mr. Wolfe held the post of constable, they might decide to take him along with them. On recognizing some of the town's leading citizens among the prisoners, Mr. Wolfe had come to the same conclusion. Tom tried to signal Mr. Wolfe to leave but was not sure if he understood him. Seconds later Tom had his answer when Mr. Wolfe addressed General Stuart again, "I can see that I will not be able to persuade you to return our horses and that am wasting my time here. With your permission, I will return to my family as they must be worried about me."

"I have no reason to keep you. Go and assure your family that both you and they are safe."

Tom happily watched Mr. Wolfe hurry from the yard and back across the bridge to town. Tom's relief lasted only seconds for when he returned his attention to the porch, he saw that General Stuart had taken a step down off it and was staring at the prisoners. What Tom heard next made him cringe.

"Private Griggs," ordered General Stuart. "I understand that you were attacked this morning."

"Yes, General Stuart," responded Private Griggs, stepping forward and saluting.

"And this is the force that attacked you?"

Nervously, Private Griggs answered, "Yes, General."

47

"I would like to hear about it."

"Yes, General."

For the next several minutes Private Griggs told his story, showing General Stuart the slingshots he had taken from the Invincibles and, as far as Tom was concerned, somewhat exaggerating what had actually happened. He made the boys stand up in a line in front of General Stuart and then told the story of the second attack that Peter had led. When Private Griggs finished, Tom decided it was time for him to act. Stepping forward he yelled, "Attention!"

The hours of drilling practice caused every one of the Invincibles, even those who were crying, to snap to attention. Tom thought he detected a slight lifting of General Stuart's mustache, as if he smiled, but could not be sure. Now he stepped forward and in a clear voice, surprisingly free of the fear he had felt just moments before, said, "Captain Thomas Jefferson Scott, commander of the Mercersburg Invincibles."

"The Mercersburg Invincibles," muttered General Stuart, before speaking more clearly. "Captain Scott, is what Private Griggs has told me, the truth? You attacked him from ambush, knocked him off his horse, and attempted to do the same to another one of my men? And then you attacked a second squad of my men?"

Tom's mouth went dry. Whatever courage he had possessed deserted him. Thankfully, Peter Bricker stepped forward. "No, it ain't! Captain Scott wasn't even there when we shot at the second bunch of infernal Confederate Rebels, and that Private feller didn't tell it right."

"Then suppose you tell it right . . .if you were there, that is."

"I was there! I was in command 'cause Captain Scott and Lieutenant Smith got captured, but not by that Private feller. He was layin' on the ground most of the fight."

General Stuart turned away for a few seconds and the other officers on the porch either did the same or lowered their heads so their faces could not be seen. When the general looked back, Peter proceeded to tell the story of the Second Battle of Mercersburg, as his fight came to be called. Tom's legs grew steadily weaker as Peter bragged about how they shot at the horses to make them buck and how the infernal Confederate Rebels went flying in all directions. Peter ended with, "And if them fellers hadn't gotten behind us, we would have run away and shot at another bunch!" Having finished, Peter stepped back into line.

For a little while General Stuart said nothing and then asked Private Griggs, "Private, let me see one of these weapons that routed a whole squad of my men."

Private Griggs handed General Stuart a slingshot. Several of the other officers asked to see one as well. After a few minutes, General Stuart ordered, "Captain Scott! Please demonstrate the use of this weapon," and handed the slingshot to Tom, who asked Private Griggs for a lead bullet. Loading the slingshot, Tom aimed at a tree down toward the creek and let fly. The loud "THWACK" came as no surprise to him, but it certainly impressed General Stuart. The general asked Private Griggs for a lead bullet, as did the other officers, and for the next five minutes slingshots twanged, lead pellets zipped, and a tree or two got thwacked. Finally, General Stuart called a halt to the target practice and again faced Tom and the Invincibles.

"These are quite remarkable, I must say, but they are also very dangerous. On this occasion, all my men have suffered were a few bruises, possibly a cracked rib or two, and some embarrassment from which their comrades will take considerable amusement in the weeks ahead. But if you had struck one of my men in the right place you could have caused him serious harm . . . or worse. Do you realize that?"

Although Tom had wanted to protect Mercersburg from the enemy, he had never seriously considered what that meant – that people, even if they were enemy soldiers, might be hurt. The idea that someone might have actually been . . . Well, he didn't want to think about that. He finally answered, "I never . . . all we wanted to do was protect our town."

"And what if my men had fired on you boys? I cannot think with what words I could have consoled your grieving mothers. Indeed, all of you were most courageous, and I admire your desire to defend your families, friends, and homes. Nevertheless, I suggest that in the future, should such circumstances again arise, that you resist the temptation to protect your town and leave such efforts to your army."

"But the army wasn't here."

"I am most grateful for that, as you should be, Captain Scott, but you represented them well and you can be proud of what you did; although, as I said, please refrain from doing it again. The outcome could be tragically different."

"Yes, Sir. We'll stick to drillin' with ax and broom handles and only shoot at tree trunks."

"Very good. Now, have your company stand at ease and do me the honor of introducing them to me."

Tom began with Jake and was half way down the line when loud shouting interrupted him. Horses began to rear and break free of their attendants as a man ran among them, obviously attempting to reach General Stuart. A number of officers leaped from the porch and helped a sergeant, commanding the general's guard detail, seize the man who continued to struggle until realizing that he could not escape. Only when the man stood in front of General Stuart did Tom recognize his father.

"I'm sorry, Gen'ral," said the sergeant. "He came up to me and asked to see you. I told 'im you couldn't see nobody, but before I could stop 'im he pushed by me and ran into the yard. He wasn't armed, Sir, so I didn't fire."

"Very well, Sergeant. It was for the best that you did not fire. We don't want to alarm the citizens."

"General Stuart!" yelled Tom. "Don't hurt him! He's my father!"

"Your father! I see. Mr. Scott, you wanted to see me. I assume it is about your son and these other boys?"

"Please, General. Don't hurt them, and please don't take them with you as prisoners. They're just boys. Take me instead of them."

"That is very honorable of you, Mr. Scott. Are you a town official?"

"No, but I . . ."

"Are you with the army and home on furlough?"

"No, I'm not in the army."

"Oh, I rather thought a man of your age . . . That matters not. You would be of no value to us, Mr. Scott. We could not exchange you for any of our people held by your government."

"But you can't take the boys!"

"Rest assured, I have no intention of taking them. In fact, your son and I have been talking about this entire affair, and I believe we have come to an understanding. Haven't we Captain Scott?"

"Yes, Sir."

"He was just introducing me to the other members of the Mercersburg Invincibles. I suppose you know what happened. These are very brave young men. You and your town should be very proud of them. Of course, as I told Captain Scott, the outcome of today's events could have been markedly different. To avoid any such future actions, I will have to ask that each of the Invincibles give their parole. My adjutant will attend to the paperwork. Once that is accomplished their sling . . . their weapons will be returned and they will be free to go."

Tom saw his father slump as if all his strength drained from him in an instant. Tom would never forget the look in his father's eyes when his father heard General Stuart's words. General Stuart continued, "Sergeant, release Mr. Scott and return to your post. If any of the other boys' parents are here, tell them what I said and assure them that they will be reunited with their sons shortly."

Tom's father stepped over to Tom and seized him by the shoulders, "I cannot imagine what you and the other boys were thinking but that doesn't matter anymore. I'll wait for you on the road until General Stuart has finished with you. We have much to talk about on the way home. Your mother was sick with worry when she heard what happened and that you had been taken prisoner. She'll be very happy and relieved to see you."

"I'm sorry, Pa."

"We'll talk about all this later."

Tom watched his father walk back to the road. He felt closer to him now than he had in many years. That feeling warmed him. But something also troubled him – something he had sensed when General Stuart had asked his father if he was a soldier home on furlough. Tom struggled to know what to do about it, but then he heard Jake ask, "What's a parole?" and his attention returned to the Invincibles and General Stuart.

"A very good question. Lieutenant Smith," responded General Stuart. "Giving your parole means that you promise not to fight again in this war until you are exchanged. In this case, it would be for any infernal Confederate Rebel boys who attack any of your soldiers with slingshots and were unfortunate enough to get themselves captured." Jake blushed at the general's use of "infernal Confederate Rebels" and General Stuart seeing it, roared with laughter.

Tom finished the introductions, and then General Stuart introduced his adjutant, Major Hairston, who was also acting as provost marshal, making him doubly suited to issue the boys their paroles. In turn each stepped up before the major, who had them swear that they would not fight until exchanged. Little Johnny Myers hesitated at first. When Major Hairston asked him why, he said, "My Ma told me never to swear, so I don't think I can." General Stuart, standing close by, struggled to contain his amusement and then explained, "Private Myers, your mother is absolutely correct. I made such a vow to my mother many years ago, but this kind of swearing means that you are making a promise. I do not believe that your mother would object, especially if it means that you will be permitted to go home to her." Johnny quickly swore his oath and lined up with the other boys. The major continued.

While the boys gave their oaths, the lady returned to the porch with some food for General Stuart and his officers. Tom heard the general say, "I thank you Mrs. Steiger for this excellent meal. I know my officers and I will enjoy it. I hope that your boys will be well soon."

When Major Hairston had given each of the Invincibles a piece of paper with his parole on it and General Stuart had finished eating, the general again stepped down off the porch and looked at Tom. "Captain Scott," he ordered, "call your company to attention."

Tom took in a huge gulp of air, puffing out his chest as he did so, and barked, "Companeee! Attention!"

"Men of the Mercersburg Invincibles," began General Stuart, "you are hereby released on your parole. It has been my pleasure to meet such gallant soldiers. Captain Scott, you may draw your weapons from Private Griggs and then march your company from the parade ground and dismiss them."

"Thank you, Sir!"

Tom's father and several of the other boys' families waited for them just north of the bridge. A great amount of hugging and kissing – along with a little ear twisting and a few words of scolding, both of which passed quickly – brought blushes to many of the Invincibles. Tom's father again took his son by the shoulders and then drew him into his arms. Tom had not been hugged by his father since . . . he couldn't remember when. Now it was Tom's turn to shed tears as he felt his father's drop on his cheek.

"Your mother will be beside herself with joy. When I left she feared the worst. We knew nothing about General Stuart, what kind of a man he was."

"I like him. Is it all right to like a Rebel?"

"Yes, of course. I'm sure he has a family too and probably misses them terribly. He is an honorable man. I'm very grateful to him for letting you go."

"I always thought the Rebels were bad, but maybe they're not as bad as I thought."

"No, perhaps not, but they still have taken many horses and mules, and who knows what Mr. Brewer and the other store owners in town have lost."

"Do you think General Stuart will let Mr. Shaffer and the other men go, like he did us?"

"No, I don't think he will. Our army has arrested many people in Virginia. He wants to exchange our people for his. I only hope that they can endure what they must pass through."

"Look, Pa, the big guns from the town square."

With a sound like a small thunderstorm, the two giant cannon rumbled over the bridge, the horses straining under the effort to increase the pace. The boys and their families scattered and watched as the gray clad troopers, many of them leading horses and mules and others with their arms full, riding horses festooned with store goods, followed the guns.

"Are they leaving?" asked Tom.

"I believe they are," answered his father.

The Johnston Run bridge had never had so many horses cross over it. How long everyone stood and watched, no one could ever recall. At last Colonel Butler appeared and reported something to General Stuart, who came out to the road to talk to him. The colonel rode away and minutes later General Stuart, now mounted, left the yard. The men who had been taken prisoner had left shortly after the Invincibles. General Stuart first turned north and then reined his horse back toward the bridge and threaded his way through the throng of cavalrymen that parted when they saw who he was. He stopped in front of Tom. "I just wanted to say good-bye. The lady of the house supplied my staff and me with a fine meal. It is well I do not live hereabouts. In a short time I should not be able to mount a horse. Captain Scott, give my regards to your men. It has been my pleasure to make your acquaintance. I doubt that we shall meet again." And with that General Stuart swept his plumed hat from his head, bowed gracefully, and disappeared into the column of marching men.

The last soldiers to leave Mercersburg were a few of the blue-coated ones, and they passed by quietly. Tom and his father stared after them and then walked back across the bridge toward Oregon

Street. Neither said anything for a time. Finally, Tom broke the silence, "I'm sorry I worried you and Ma so. Everything happened so fast. One minute we were hidin' behind some bushes, and the next we were standin' up and firin' at the soldiers."

"It doesn't matter now. You and the other boys are safe."

"Did the Rebels come out to our farm?"

"Yes, they did."

"So all of our horses and mules are gone."

"No, they're not."

"But . . . but how. Did you fight the Rebels?"

"No . . . no, there was no need. When they came the horses and mules were gone."

"Gone?"

"Yes, I was busy in the barn getting things ready for the threshing this afternoon. The next thing I know, Ruth is tugging at my pants leg. I looked down at her and she said, 'Hide horses.' She didn't say another word but turned around and left the barn. She stood at the door and pointed out toward the gully down by the creek. Now, as you know, your sister says precious little. She talks to me more than she does to everybody else put together, and when she says something I have learned to listen very carefully to what she says. Something told me that this was one time I had better do more than just listen. So I took all the animals down to the gully. I had scarcely returned and called your mother and Ruth into the barn when four gray-coated men rode up the road. We hid in the loft. They looked all around and called out, but we didn't answer. They tried to take some of the chickens, but that crazed rooster of ours wouldn't let them in the coop. Then they rode off."

Tom told his father about what Ruth had done that morning,

56

ending with, "How does she know these things, Pa?"

"I don't know. Maybe it's like the way animals know a storm's coming or the feeling a person sometime gets about a relation being ill or hurt, only stronger. It's a mystery to your Ma and me."

"How'd you know about me and what happened?"

"Mr. Winger came and told us. Said he'd seen you in town under guard. I got so excited I grabbed the harness to hitch up the horses before I remembered where they were and that I didn't dare ride one into town. So I started to walk. When I reached town some of the people still on the square told me where the Rebels had taken you."

"And you came to get me and woulda taken my and the other boys' places."

"It was all I could think of to do."

"Pa, you ain't no coward. I saw how you looked when General Stuart asked about you being a soldier home on furlough. You looked like you believed he thought you were."

"I don't rightly know what I thought or felt, Tom. I suppose that General Stuart might think I'm a coward but that doesn't matter. What the people of this town think of me does. And it matters more every day, especially this day."

"Are you goin' to ask Ma to give you your promise back?"

"Give my promise back? I never heard it put just that way before. I have a great deal of thinkin' to do, and your Ma and me have a great deal of talkin' to do."

"Do you want to join the army?"

"I don't know that it's so much a want as a need. When I saw all those Rebels in town today, I thought of how terrified everyone was. I don't know that my bein' in the army would've made any difference on the Rebels comin' here or not. But if every man does

57

his duty in this war, then maybe it will be over sooner."

Suddenly, Tom realized that they were walking down the road to their farm and his mother was running toward him, laughing and crying at the same time. Then a great amount of hugging and kissing – along with a little ear twisting and a few words of scolding, both of which passed quickly – made Tom blush. He felt something at his legs and looking down saw Ruth, holding onto him with all her might.

CHAPTER 4

Giving Back a Promise

For the rest of the day, Tom's mother would not let him out of her sight. She took turns hugging and kissing him and then scolding him for his "foolish" actions. Ruth clung to him, holding either his hand or a pants leg and following him around like a new puppy. Tom's father said very little. He smiled when his wife said something about Tom and the other boys being safe and sound, but otherwise kept silent and to himself. Tom understood that his father had said all he wanted to say about what had happened. Something else ate at him, and Tom knew exactly what it was.

Mercersburg was in turmoil for the next several days. Even though the Rebels had departed as quietly and as peacefully as they had come, not a shot - except for Mr. Shaffer's - being fired, their stay in the town had turned it upside down. Gone forever was the feeling of safety and security that had pervaded the town before the coming of the Rebels. The war, once something that touched a few of the citizens from a distance through friends or relatives in the army, had visited them at their very doorsteps. As long as any of them lived, they would never forget it. The toll on the town included eight men carried off as prisoners. Their unknown fate haunted those who knew them. Several other town officials had barely managed to escape capture. Nearly every farmer along the line of the Rebels'

59

march had lost two or more horses; one as many as eighteen. The shelves of every store in town lay all but bare, while the store owners held a fistful of worthless Confederate money or payment notes. The Rebels had not left without a parting warning that 20,000 of their infantry would soon follow them. The tale, soon proven to be false, nevertheless frightened many.

The day after Stuart and his cavalry left town, Tom and his father drove in their wagon back into Mercersburg. Tom had not wanted to go, not knowing what kind of treatment he could expect. As they entered Franklin Street, a few of the townspeople ran by yelling that the Rebels had returned. On nearing the square, Tom saw horsemen coming down the street. Panic gripped him but soon faded. This cavalry belonged to the Union. Captain John W. Russell and his forty men looked weary. Tom thought that they should be glad they had not been in Mercersburg the previous day. What could forty men have hoped to have done against the thousands that marched with General Stuart?

Tom saw that his father had a great deal of explaining to do about how he had managed to keep his horses. For once the people of the town talked to him, though only long enough to get his story. Tom saw Jake and called to him. Jake came up, shaking his head from side to side. "I tell you. It was all I could do to get away from my ma this morning. She 'bout done for me last night, squeezin' me one minute and pullin' my ear almost off the next. I hear that Billy got a whuppin' and then his ma made 'im his favorite meal. What happened to you?"

"'Bout the same. No whuppin' though. Hear 'bout any of the others?"

"Naw. Reckon they got what we got or what Billy got or both. How come you still got horses?"

"Ruth."

60

"That sister of yours has some strange ways 'bout her, but I guess they come in handy sometimes."

"Yeah."

Some ladies stopped right in front of Tom and Jake and gaped at them for a minute. Finally one said, "You two were with those boys who nearly got taken off as prisoners for fighting with the Rebels, weren't you?"

Tom didn't know what to say, but Jake spoke right up, "Yes ma'am, we are, and we gave them infernal Confederate Rebels a good lickin'."

"Your parents should have kept you at home. You put the entire town in danger. I have it on good authority that the Rebel General Stuart almost carted off the entire bunch of you along with your mothers, brothers, sisters, and the fathers who are too old to serve in the army or just haven't seen fit to volunteer yet. Who else might they have taken? I shudder to think."

Tom bristled and was about to argue back, but Jake beat him to it.

"That's not true!"

"Well, we can see by your manners what kind of upbringing you have had. No wonder you did such a foolish thing." Then the two women walked away hurriedly, complaining loudly about the bad manners of some children.

"Do you think the whole town feels that way 'bout what we done?" asked Tom.

"Don't know. I got a feelin' that we'll find out though."

The word about how the Scotts held onto their horses swept through Mercersburg in less time than it took to take a breath. Tom's father told only about a half-dozen people, but within an hour people stopped asking him about his horses and started to treat him like they had before. The worst part of the day came on their way home. Johnny Myers's mother ran up to them. Tom's father pulled the horses to a stop.

"Jonathan Scott!" Mrs. Myers yelled, causing several people to stop and gawk at her. "Your son nearly cost me my boy. I don't know whether you knew what Tom was up to, but you should have. He's no good if you ask me. You keep him away from Johnny in the future, you hear, or I'll have words with Constable Wolfe." Mrs. Myers stormed off, tears rolling down her cheeks.

"I'm sorry Pa," Tom managed to say, once he got control of his voice.

"She's just upset, but I think you should stay away from Johnny for a while . . . and maybe the rest of the boys too. From the little that people said to me in town, feelings are pretty divided as to whether you boys did a courageous thing or a foolish thing. I know which one your mother believes, and I suppose all the other boys' mothers would agree with her."

"I guess that's the end of the Invincibles then."

"The Invincibles?"

"We called ourselves the Mercersburg Invincibles. We thought we could protect the town."

"And what do you think now?"

"I guess Ma's right and Johnny's mother, too."

"Don't take it too hard, Thomas. Our leaders thought this war would be over in three months. They're not boys, but grown men. They should have known better. In fact, they should have found a way to avoid the war altogether."

"What are you goin' to do 'bout the war, Pa?"

"Don't know just yet. For a minute there today, I thought all was returning to the way it had been, but it didn't last. The people still . . ."

"They still won't talk to you?"

"No. Let's say no more about it for now."

Tom learned the next day that even more Union soldiers had come into town after Captain Russell had left. Some of them ate with Dr. Creigh, the Presbyterian minister of the church the Scotts attended, and his family. More cavalry arrived the next day, bringing the news that General Stuart and his men, along with horses and prisoners, had somehow eluded the Union forces and escaped over the Potomac River back into Virginia. Tom didn't show it, at least he hoped he didn't, but a part of him was happy. While he still feared the infernal Confederate Rebels, he felt that he had made a friend of one of them. He was happy that one was safe.

On Sunday, the family attended church services at the Presbyterian Church and listened to Dr. Creigh speak. At first, Tom was surprised at all the people in attendance, but after he thought about it, he understood completely. He had trouble keeping his mind on Dr. Creigh's words, and instead of concentrating on them, continuously glanced this way and that to see if anyone was looking at him. He didn't catch anyone actually staring, but couldn't escape the feeling that he was being watched. His head swiveled this way and that so often his mother elbowed him on the arm to make him stop. He spent the last half of the service sitting stiffly erect, head forward. As he left the church, Tom could feel eyes on him and heard several people whispering things like, "That's one of those boys," or, "I heard he's always been a trouble maker." Rebecca Scott heard them too and responded by placing her arm on her son's shoulders and hurrying him toward their wagon. They rode home in silence.

As if Mercersburg had not seen enough cavalry, four days after General Stuart's 2,000 plus men invaded the town, another 2,500 came through. Again those in the lead wore blue uniforms. The people of Mercersburg took a collective breath and held it until they saw that all the rest of the soldiers also wore the blue of the Union.

Like Stuart, these cavalrymen traveled the road to Chambersburg. Tom got to see them march over the same arched bridge where he had stood when the Rebels had left Mercersburg. He had again accompanied his father into town. This time Jonathan Scott had come not to talk or purchase but to vote. While Tom waited, Jake, Billy, and Peter, whose fathers had come to town to do the same, gathered around him.

"I hear you got a whuppin'," Tom said to Billy.

"I had worse. My ma gave me a couple of good swats. Didn't know she could. Pa always whupped me before when I needed it."

"Your Pa whup you, Peter?" asked Tom.

"Nah. My ma wouldn't let go of me long enough for my Pa to get a hold on me. But you know, yesterday, Ma finally let me out of the house, and Pa caught me and took me into the barn. I thought for sure I was goin' to get it, but instead he says, 'Peter. You did a wild and foolish thing. For a time I didn't know what to think of it, but the more I thought on it the more I come to think that you did a brave thing, still foolish mind you, but very, very brave. I'm proud of you!' Honest, I tell you that was what he said. I swear."

"A couple of my pa's friends," added Jake, "told him the same thing 'bout us. They said we was heroes, genuine heroes. Some others said that we should all get a good whuppin' on account of puttin' the whole town in danger."

"I guess," Tom puzzled, "half the town thinks we're heroes and the other half thinks we need a good whuppin'."

"I hope I can figure out which half is which," chuckled Peter.

Then Billy raised the question that had bounced around in all their heads over the last few days. "Are the Invincibles ever goin' to meet again?"

"Do you want to?" ask Tom. "Do you think we should? If the half of the town that wants to whup us finds out, we'll catch it good."

"How'll they find out?" argued Jake. "They didn't know 'bout us all the other times. If none of us gives it away, they won't know 'bout it this time neither."

Tom had given up all thoughts of the Invincibles ever meeting again. He believed that the boys, like he, had been scared so badly that they would never want to pick up an ax or broom handle, much less a slingshot, ever again. Yet here three of them stood, urging him to call the Invincibles together once more. He was still their captain. They looked to him to lead them. Their eager faces stared at him, eyes wide with expectation. How could he say no? He didn't want to say no, even though he knew he should. Before he realized it his mouth opened and out popped the words, "We'll meet by the old tree along the creek next Monday after morning chores. Tell the rest of the boys, except for Johnny."

"My pa took my slingshot," muttered Billy.

"I'm sure some of the others lost theirs too," volunteered Jake.

"It's okay," Tom heard himself say. "I can make more. I got extra rubber."

All the way home, a battle raged inside Tom's head. One side argued that he must be crazy to bring the Invincibles together again after what happened. The other side argued that what had happened could never happen again in a thousand years, so the Invincibles could never get into trouble again. He was thankful that his father remained quiet, never wondering why, or else he might have blurted out what he was thinking about. By the time he stepped down off the wagon his head hurt. It continued to hurt right through supper and then it hurt even more.

After supper, as was the family's custom, everyone shared their news of the day. Jonathan revealed that there was rumor that Mr.

Blair and Mr. Raby had escaped from the Rebels and were on their way back to Mercersburg. The good news quickly faded when Tom's mother revealed that she had received another letter from her brother. Tom glanced at his father. No wonder he had said nothing all the way home. He had the letter in his pocket. Now Tom understood that the letter had weighed on his father as much as the Invincibles had weighed on him. He tried not to watch his father's face but couldn't look away.

Rebecca Scott read the letter. Uncle Jeremiah wrote about all the things he had been doing from guard duty to the never ending drilling. He told of how proud he was to be with his regiment because of the good reputation it had. With every word, Tom saw his father's face darken until at last, "Enough Rebecca!" Jonathan Scott cried. Rebecca blanched white. Tom nearly fell out of his chair. Ruth held up her doll, looked at Tom, and whispered, "Go outside." She grabbed Tom's hand and pulled him to his feet. The next minute they were sitting on the porch step.

As he sat there in the twilight, his sister nestling up close to him, Tom could hear clearly the words that wafted through the partly opened window next to him. He didn't want to listen to them, but he could not help but hear.

"Rebecca," Tom heard his father plead. "Rebecca, I can no longer sit quietly and listen to those letters. I know that Jeremiah does not mean to write anything hurtful, but his words are like stones hitting me. I cannot bear to hear what he says about his regiment and his pride in it. I no longer have any pride in myself. The people of this town shun me. My friends avoid me. I have heard that because of the Rebels coming through here, John Mowery is planning to enlist. John has many obligations and what he does here at home is more valuable to the war than what he will do as a soldier. But he is going, and because of the promise I made to you, I cannot."

"Then you want me to release you? I tell you I can't. I won't. You know why I made you make that promise. What has changed? Jeremiah is still in the army, still in danger. I will not risk you as well."

"Rebecca! Can't you see what this is doing to me?"

"I know what it is doing to you and I care about it. But I care about you more. Here with us you are alive. If I let you go . . . Jonathan, I could not bear to see your name on one of those lists posted outside the hotel. I have seen what those lists do to people. I could not bear it."

Tom could not stand to hear any more. Pulling Ruth to her feet, he took her hand and walked toward the barn. He searched within himself, trying to find his own feelings about it all. He knew his father was no coward, but many in the town thought he was. One by one, his father's closest friends had stopped coming by to visit. Even his mother's friends had begun to stay away from her. How long before Jake and the rest of the Invincibles started staying away from him? He looked down at Ruth. He wondered if she understood. As if to answer him she stared up into his face and said, "Pa will be a soldier soon."

"How do you know that?"

"Pa will be a soldier soon."

They sat in a pile of straw for nearly half an hour. Muffled sounds from the house drifted to them. Ruth played with her doll. Tom lay back, thinking all sorts of things, none of them pleasant. At last the back door opened. His mother called to him. Together, he and Ruth walked slowly back to the house. For once it appeared that Ruth was wrong. Jonathan Scott did not leave. He did not go off to join the army. His oath still anchored him to family and farm. The subject did not come up again for the rest of the week, and on the next Monday,

Tom had his own problems to deal with.

Full of nervous energy, Tom rushed through his chores, still hating them, but resigned to doing them so as not to give his father any more worries than those he had already. Tom arrived first at the meeting spot. He had managed to make three more slingshots and hoped that would be all he would need for the present. The Invincibles started to arrive about twenty minutes later. Jake, the first, plopped down next to Tom. "Did like you ordered. Told all the boys except for Johnny. Don't know how many will show up."

Over the next fifteen minutes they had the answer. Nine out of the twelve arrived, one at a time or in pairs. As usual Peter was the last. All carried an ax or broom handle, and all but two had their slingshots. They sat around Tom, not saying a word, waiting for their captain to speak. Finally Tom got up enough nerve to stand and call out, "Attention Invincibles! Fall in!" While the line formed he fought to find words to say. In the end, he just started talking.

"Stand at ease. Do your parents know where you are?" A smattering of "No" and some accompanying head shaking told him that none did. "I didn't think we'd ever meet again after what happened. I thought most of you would be mad at me for getting you into all that trouble. I got to be honest with you. I formed the Invincibles only so I could boss you around. I never thought we'd have to fight anybody."

Jake took it on himself to reply for all. "We didn't neither . . . think that we'd have to fight, I mean. You bully everybody anyway so that part didn't matter. We just wanted to play at being soldiers and you gave us the chance. Besides you knew more about it than we did."

For the next hour one by one the boys told of their experiences during and after the Rebels rode through Mercersburg. All admitted to being terrified when they got captured. Gradually Tom's worries disappeared - along with the way he had always felt about his "friends." Up until now he had always looked on them as being targets for his own amusement. He had enjoyed watching them all shake when he came near. He never considered them real friends, including Jake. In fact, until the events of the past few days, he had not known what a real friend was. What he and they had been through together had changed that; and him.

Tom said very little more; a real change. Instead he led the Invincibles in drills and target practice. Just as they were about to break up and go home to eat dinner, Johnny Myers appeared. Tom froze. Jake stepped between them, saying to Johnny, "How'd you know 'bout us meetin'?"

"Didn't know. Just sorta wandered down here. Hi, Tom."

"You can't be here," Tom said, nervously looking around to see if Mrs. Myers had followed her son. "Your ma said I ain't to be anywhere near you or she'll get Constable Wolfe after me."

"She don't know I'm here, and I don't think she meant what she said. She was just mad and scared 'bout me."

"But if she did mean it?"

"I'll tell her I met you by accident."

"You better go, Johnny."

"I wanna stay. I'm sorry I wasn't as brave as the rest of you. I shouldn't've cried. Invincibles don't cry."

"You weren't the only one to cry. I did too."

"You, Tom? You cried!"

"Yeah, I did. Most of us did. You weren't any more scared than the rest of us."

"Then can I get back into the Invincibles? I still got my slingshot."

"You mean that after everything that happened you still want to be in the Invincibles?"

"It was the most fun I ever had."

Tom tried very hard to fight it, but the look on Johnny's face finally defeated him, and he burst out laughing. One by one the other boys followed - Johnny, at first not sure what was so funny, being the last. Finally the laughter died away and the rippling sound of Johnston Run could be heard once again. Having collapsed to the ground, everyone lay still and quiet for several minutes, each with his own thoughts. Johnny broke the silence with, "Well, can I get back in?"

Tom raised himself on his elbows, and stared Johnny in the face before answering, "You were never out."

On the surface Mercersburg recovered from its frightful experience more rapidly than anyone could have imagined – except for the horses that had been taken. Replacing them would take some time. For once a rumor proved true. Mr. Blair and Mr. Raby had escaped, and before long the *Good Intent* was being publishing once again. Amazingly, the last October issue of the paper didn't mention the Rebels at all. Tom wasn't much for paper reading, but he wondered how everyone could have forgotten the invasion so quickly, or did they simply not want to be reminded about it. But even though the town as a whole may have ceased to dwell on the unpleasant visit, Tom was well aware that it still haunted some people – his father being one of them.

Through the early part of November the Scott home, like an old weaving, slowly began to unravel. Tom's parents talked less and less to each other. His father left early in the morning, more often than not carrying his dinner with him. Suppers were short with no sharing of the day's news afterward. Tom quickly discovered that his father did his own work and Tom's chores as well – anything to keep him away from the house. Tom's mother saw fewer and fewer visitors drop by, and she went nowhere, leaving the house only when her work took her outside. If Tom accompanied his father to town on an errand or business, they said nothing to each other. Tom didn't know what to say, and his father just gazed off into the distance. Only Ruth weathered the storm. Doll in hand she became the only light in the darkness for both her mother and her father, and one afternoon near the middle of the month she healed everyone.

Tom never forgot that day. He had a meeting of the Invincibles in the morning after chores, and stepped out of the back door to see his father already doing one of them, scattering feed to the chickens. His mother hung up clothes to dry on a line a few yards from the porch. As Tom stood and watched the two of them, Ruth came out the back door, looked up at Tom, and smiled. She handed him her doll and said, "Please hold Amy." Wondering at the strange request, Tom took the doll and at that moment the wash line broke, dropping almost all his mother's clean clothes on the dusty ground. Rebecca Scott fell to her knees, her face in her hands, weeping. His back toward the house Jonathan did not see what had happened. The next thing Tom knew, Ruth stood next to her mother. She gently took one of her mother's hands and whispered something Tom could not hear. Rebecca rose to her feet, and with Ruth guiding her she walked toward her husband.

Jonathan Scott reached down to get more feed but instead found his daughter's tiny hand. Tom saw his father look at Ruth, only then realizing that Rebecca was with her. Ruth, now holding the hands of both her parents, looked up at them and joined their hands. She said something Tom could not hear and then ran toward him. The next thing he knew she was asking him, "May I have Amy back please?" He gave her the doll. She took his hand, said, "Pa will be a soldier now," and pulled him through the door into the kitchen.

71

After that morning everything changed. Rebecca Scott gave her husband's promise back to him, and the two of them worked side by side, along with Tom and sometimes Ruth, to prepare the farm not only for the winter but also Jonathan's leaving. The news that Jonathan Scott would soon be off to join the army spread rapidly through Mercersburg. Once again, he walked with his head held high, his eyes meeting those of his neighbors. Still hurt by their actions, he spoke little to them at first, but gradually he became his old self.

Once most of the farm work had been completed, Jonathan took a trip to Chambersburg to see an army enlistment officer. Rebecca, Tom, and Ruth waved to him from the front porch as he drove away. Rebecca, tears coursing down her cheeks, quickly went inside once the wagon disappeared from view down the lane. Tom jumped from the porch and ran off toward Johnston Run and another secret meeting of the Invinvcibles. Ruth remained, her eyes gazing into the distance after her father.

All the Invincibles waited for Tom by the old tree. They were much different from the old Invincibles before the Rebels came to Mercersburg. These Invincibles, battle tested, had been forged by their experience into a solid band of friends. Tom no longer bullied any of them, and only in the line of duty did he order them around. In fact, he often didn't do that, allowing Jake to put the company through its drills. Even newly promoted Sergeant Peter Bricker took a turn one memorable afternoon. He became overly excited, forgetting to order a halt, and half of the company ended up in the creek. Further drilling that day became impossible and instead a massive water fight erupted, leaving both officers and privates wet and exhausted from their efforts and their laughter. Fortunately, the day had been somewhat warm, one of the last of an Indian summer that embraced Mercersburg.

Now, on this day, Tom stood by and let Jake drill the company. Tom's thoughts flitted back and forth from his father leaving to the new life he had to face as the "man" of the family. While helping his father one afternoon in the barn, Jonathan pulled Tom down on an upside-down feed bucket, took a seat on an overturned water bucket next to him, and talked to him about taking his place on the farm. The more his father talked the less Tom wanted him to leave. The whole idea of running the farm through the winter and then tackling spring planting, quickly made him want to talk his father out of joining the army. Now, as he watched the Invincibles drill, a thought popped into his head. It remained there ever so briefly before being knocked to one side by Jake yelling at Billy for being out of step. He was still having problems remembering his left foot from his right. But the thought did not go far, and it came to Tom later that night as he tried to go to sleep – *Why couldn't he go with his father and become a drummer boy?* Tom decided to keep the idea to himself, knowing what the answer would be if he ever asked to be allowed to go.

Tom's father returned the next day, having joined the same regiment and company as his wife's brother. Rebecca had insisted on this so that each man could watch out for the other. From the bounty money that was paid to Jonathan Scott when he enlisted, the family would have enough to help them through the following year and, if they had a good crop the next harvest, beyond.

While he had been in Chambersburg, Jonathan had gone to a photographer and had his picture taken in a uniform that the photographer kept on hand for just such occasions. Rebecca placed the small, framed tintype on the mantel above the fireplace in the sitting room. It vanished the next day. A frantic search ended when Ruth was found sitting on the back porch, staring at it. Rebecca returned it to the mantel and told Ruth to leave it there. From time to time over the following months the image would disappear again and again until Rebecca noticed that it was gone. It was always found with Ruth. Finally, Rebecca gave up and allowed Ruth to carry it wherever she wished.

The day finally came for Jonathan to report for duty. The whole family rode in the wagon to Colonel Murphy's hotel where the coach line dropped off and picked up its passengers. Much to Jonathan's surprise, a good-sized crowd of Mercersburg's finer citizens had gathered to give him a send-off. As he stepped down off the wagon, several men came forward and shook his hand. Others slapped him on the back. Remembering how these same people had treated his father before, Tom climbed down off the other side of the wagon, not wanting to have to talk to any of them. Unluckily, Johnny Myers and his mother came walking across the street directly toward him. Tom looked for an escape route and was about to bolt when his mother asked him to help her and Ruth down from the wagon seat. By the time he turned to go, Mrs. Myers stood right in front of him.

"Hello, Mrs. Scott," she said. "I know how you feel today. I said good-bye to my husband on this very spot over two years ago."

"Yes," Rebecca replied. "I remember that day very well."

"You came to be with me. I felt it my duty to do the same for you."

"I thank you, Sarah."

"I . . . I said some very harsh words to your husband and your son after . . . after the Rebels . . ."

"It was a very difficult time for all of us."

"I should not have said them. My Johnny was as much to blame as any of the other boys. I'd like very much to invite you to visit me and please bring your children."

Tom's legs nearly gave way. Johnny had a smile a mile wide on his face and threw Tom a knowing wink. They had been "visiting" each other for weeks.

"Why, thank you Sarah. I . . . we would enjoy that very much, wouldn't we Thomas?"

An elbow nudge brought out a "Yes, thank you," from him.

The embarrassing moment ended as the coach rolled to a stop, breaking up the crowd. Two men got out of the coach, and Jonathan stepped forward to enter it. Rebecca, Tom, and Ruth surrounded him; Ruth hugging his legs, Tom his chest, and Rebecca his neck. Jonathan kissed his wife and then took Tom's hand and shook it, saying, "I'm depending on you. You're the man of the family now." As he picked up Ruth, she pulled the tintype out from her doll's apron and held it up next to her father's face. "It looks just like you, Pa. I'll keep you with me all the time."

"You do just that, Ruthy."

The next moment he entered the coach, closed the door, and in a clattering of hooves and a small cloud of dust, was gone.

CHAPTER 5

Winter

The ride home took no longer than any other. It just seemed so. Rebecca drove the horses with one hand and dabbed at her eyes, using part of her shawl, with the other. Tom had wanted to drive, but his mother still thought he was too young to handle a team of horses by himself. Oh, he could hitch and unhitch them, comb them, feed and water them, and in fact do everything necessary to care for them, but he could not drive them. He had visions of his mother following along behind the plow next spring while he stood by watching. Some farmer he would make. His father had told him that he would be the "man" of the family. Tom understood that would happen only if his mother allowed him to be.

Winter came on slowly. Tom had always hated winter. True, he thoroughly enjoyed the sledding, the snowball battles, and Christmas, as any boy his age would, but the cold kept him home too much. He felt trapped in a box. He didn't really mind the cold, but his mother believed that sickness hid in every snowflake and was determined to keep her children as warm and dry as humanly possible. At first this winter was no different from any other, until his mother began to realize that with her husband gone, everything had changed. The comfortable routines the family had been used to vanished along with Jonathan, when the coach pulled away from

77

Colonel Murphy's hotel. She soon came to grasp the truth – she could not run the farm alone. She needed Tom. That meant he spent less time in school, which had started up again. So did many of the other children, especially the boys. The lack of horses on the farms surrounding Mercersburg meant more work for human backs and legs.

Even though there were no crops to plant and tend during the winter, there was still much to do on the farm. Equipment needed repair. Animals required attentive care. Little tasks that had been put off, like fastening loose boards on the chicken coop, greasing axles, sharpening tools, and a host of other things had to be done to prepare for spring. Little by little, as the mass of work began to overwhelm her, Rebecca gave her son more and more to do. Gradually, as his workload increased, Tom longed for the days when he was just a "boy" and not a "man." As far as he could see, the only good thing to come from his "growing up" was that he got out of the house.

The time eventually came when Tom's mother could no longer put off visiting Mrs. Myers. With Christmas just three weeks away, Rebecca bundled up Ruth until only her eyes were visible, nagged Tom into his heaviest coat, hat, and muffler, and called on Mrs. Myers. Sitting around staring at each other in front of a roaring fire plunged Tom into the depths of boredom. Johnny rescued him, suggesting they go out and see the new horses his mother recently bought to replace those taken by the Rebels. Once out of the house, Tom confessed, "I'm sure glad you thought of this, Johnny. If I had to stay in there one more minute . . ."

"Me, too. Did you get a letter from your pa yet?"

"No. Ma says he's probably too busy learnin' how to be a soldier to write."

"My pa didn't write for three whole months after he joined the army. Ma was really worried 'bout him. But then she got a letter and felt better. Do you miss your pa? I miss mine."

"Yeah, I miss him."

"Are the Invincibles goin' to meet soon? I'm gettin' out of practice with my slingshot."

Tom had been working so hard on the farm he hadn't thought about the Invincibles for weeks. He had seen the other boys in school, on those days he had been able to attend, but all were as busy as he was. "I'd sure like to, but everybody has so much work to do."

"Well, we've got all winter to do it. Maybe we could all sneak out every couple of days and do some drillin' and target shootin'."

Johnny's suggestion stuck with Tom the rest of the day and into the next. The more he thought about it, the more he wanted to do it. He formulated plan after plan on how he could slip away from the farm and meet with the boys for an afternoon. By the end of the week, he had determined to put his latest one into operation that very Sunday after church services.

All through Dr. Creigh's sermon, Tom ran over his plan. Carefully, so his mother would not take notice, he glanced around the sanctuary, looking for the Invincibles. He counted six. Hoping to meet with as many as he could, he dashed out of the church as soon as Dr. Creigh finished his final prayer. Tom managed to nab Peter and Billy together. He explained his plan and they immediately agreed to it. They ran off to find two of the other boys while Tom looked for Jake. The Invincibles' lieutenant agreed to the plan almost before Tom finished explaining it, complaining, "I'm wearin' my hands out. Come spring they'll be stubs. I think I've been crunched down a couple of inches with all the carryin' I've done. I tell you, Tom. There won't be nothin' left of Jake Smith by the time this winter's over."

Tom stifled a laugh, not wanting to call any attention to their conversation. "Peter and Billy are spreadin' the word. Now remember, on Tuesday tell your ma that you need to go into town for somethin'. We'll meet at the same place as before. When we're finished we'll all tell our parents that we had to go to all the stores to try and find what we wanted, but none of them had it."

"It's a good plan, but what'll we say the next time?"

"We'll work that out when we meet. Maybe we'll just say that we have some fence repairin' to do or somethin' like that. Then we can leave and meet."

"I got to hand it to you, Tom. You sure can make good plans to get out of workin'."

"I've had lots of practice."

Tom had not expected that every member of the Invincibles would be able to make the meeting, and they didn't. But ten did, and the afternoon flew by. All the boys agreed that they had been worked too hard and determined to do anything to get away so they could meet a couple of times a week. Not one felt a pinch of guilt.

Jonathan Scott's first letter arrived eight days before Christmas. News of the great battle at Fredericksburg had thrown Rebecca Scott into a panic. The letter greatly comforted her. Jonathan's regiment had not been in the battle, but actually stood by watching. Both Jonathan and Jeremiah were safe. Tom's father had spent very little time training before being ordered to join his regiment. Much that he learned about "soldiering" he learned from Jeremiah. Like his brother-in-law, Jonathan drilled and drilled and drilled. His health, even in the cold weather, was good. That night Tom heard his mother crying in her room. He promised himself that he would stop meeting with the Invincibles and dedicate himself to the farm. His promise lasted through Christmas – mostly because the Invincibles held no meetings.

Tom could not remember all the Christmases of his life, but all those that he could remember had included his father. Up until that morning, he had missed his father because of all the work that had to be done on the farm - work that his father used to do that he now had to do. On this morning, Tom missed him because he loved him. His mother, Ruth, and he decorated the tree without the usual joy they had had on other Christmases. Ruth stopped several times, went off by herself, pulled out her father's picture from the folds of her doll's dress, and stared longingly at it. Her mother saw her but did not scold her for taking the picture from the mantle. Instead, she hugged her and sat with her, both of them looking at it. Tom finished the decorating and ran outside to feed the chickens.

From that day on, everything Tom did around the farm reminded him of his father - every tool he sharpened, every swipe of the currycomb, every chore he did. Each letter that arrived kept him spellbound as his mother read it. Out of sheer desperation he broke his promise and called more meetings of the Invincibles, just to escape the farm. Sometimes only two or three boys showed up. Nevertheless, Tom continued to call the meetings, neglecting more and more of his farm work. Then at one of the meetings Ben Rankin came with a small barrel he had fixed up to be a drum, asking if he could beat it while the Invincibles marched. Although he couldn't really do more than beat out a time, the boys enjoyed it. For Tom it brought back an old idea that he had tucked away in his mind weeks before.

One of Uncle Jeremiah's letters had mentioned his regiment's drummer boys. At the time Tom had paid little attention to it, but now he wanted to know as much about those drummer boys as possible. One day he sneaked into his mother's room and searched through the letters until he found the right one. He read the paragraph about the drummer boys over and over again until he had memorized it. Tom never really remembered the moment he made his decision, only that after he made it he became determined to act on it. He would run away to the army and join his father's regiment as a drummer boy.

Once the thrill of his idea wore off a little, Tom found his thoughts focusing on what would happen to his mother and Ruth after he had gone. They certainly could not run the farm without his help. That had already been proven. His grand plan developed cracks that his guilt filled in and made larger. Torn between wanting to be with his father and his duty to remain with his mother and work the farm, Tom became short-tempered and miserable. On a trip into Mercersburg with his mother, he started a fight in Brewer's store over nothing more than an accidental bump involving a smaller boy that caused Tom to drop one of the packages he was carrying. The little scrap actually solved two problems. First, it helped relieve all his tension, and second it brought an answer to the difficulty that had been causing it.

During the wrestling and punch throwing, Tom knocked over a small oil lamp, breaking the glass. After Mr. Brewer separated the two boys, Tom's mother insisted on paying for the lamp. As she gave Mr. Brewer the money, a thought flashed into Tom's head. His mother had money – more money than the family ever had had before. He had completely forgotten about his father's enlistment bonus. There was enough money to hire a worker to help his mother with the spring plowing and planting. She didn't need him after all.

82

Tom never heard a word of the scolding his mother gave him during the ride home. All he could think about was that he could now leave home and not worry about his mother and Ruth.

The intense cold of January and February, school, and farm chores finally brought the meetings of the Invincibles to an end. From time to time Tom saw most of the boys at school, at church, or in town whenever he had to go there to purchase items for his mother or for his work around the farm. On a nail buying expedition in late February, he met Jake in Mr. Shannon's store. By that time Tom had finished his plan for running away, although he had yet to decide when he would leave. Having kept everything a secret, he longed to tell someone about it. On several occasions he almost blurted it out when sitting with a few of the Invincibles at school eating their mid-day meal. Luckily, he managed to swallow his words before they passed his lips, but this time he wasn't fast enough.

"Jake. I got somethin' to tell you, but you got to promise not to tell nobody nothin' 'bout it. If you do, I'll thrash you good."

Jake smiled. "You'll try to thrash me good, but you know it will be a tough go."

"Awwww! You know what I mean. You can't tell nobody what I'm goin' to tell you. Promise?"

"Okay. I promise."

"I'm goin' to run away and join my Pa in the army."

Had Tom been able to make a tintype of the look on Jake's face, it would have kept him laughing for decades to come. Eyes larger than two full moons, mouth open wide enough to eat an apple whole, pale as a ghost, Jake stood frozen to the spot unable to move or breathe. At last, Tom took him by both shoulders and shook him until he gasped for air. After a few seconds he managed to utter a few words, "Do you . . . mean it?"

83

"Course I mean it."

More recovered now, Jake argued back, "But you can't."

"Sure I can. I got it all worked out."

"But you're too young to be a soldier."

"I'm old enough to be a drummer boy."

A look of understanding flashed across Jake's face. "A drummer boy. You know how to drum?"

"No, but they'll teach me once my pa tells them to."

"You'd leave your ma and sister without anyone to help them on the farm?"

"Pa got money for joinin' the army. That'll pay for help with the plowin' and plantin' come spring."

"You been thinkin' 'bout this a lot. Ain't you?"

"Yeah. I really miss my pa and want to be with him. Ma has Ruth, but Pa ain't got nobody."

"I thought your ma's brother was in the same regiment."

"He is, but it ain't like havin' your own family with you."

"No, I guess not. When you leavin'?"

"Ain't decided yet. When the weather's better. Now, you won't tell nobody. Right?"

"Naw, I'll not tell."

And Jake kept his word. It was Tom who accidentally spilled his whole plot to Peter Bricker. It happened in early March. A few days of milder weather caused Tom to call a meeting of the Invincibles down by the old tree along Johnston Run on a Saturday afternoon. It being the first meeting of the year, Tom arrived very early only to find Peter sitting with his back against the tree. Plopping down beside him, Tom started talking about the Invincibles. He chattered away without thinking until . . . "You and Jake will have to do the drilling once I'm gone off to . . ."

84

"You leavin'?" interrupted Peter. "Where you goin'?"

Tom panicked and tried to bluff his way out. "Me? Leavin'? Where you get that from?"

"From you. Just now you said you was leavin'. Your ma goin' to sell the farm?"

"No, I didn't! No, she's not!"

"Sure you did. Hey! What's goin' on with you? Why will Jake and me have to do the drillin'?"

Realizing that he could not convince Peter otherwise and not wanting to be talking about it when the other boys started to arrive, Tom gave up. "I'm goin' to run away and join the army to be with my pa. But you can't tell nobody. Only Jake and you know."

"But what 'bout your ma and the farm?"

"I got that all figured out. Now don't say nothin'. Here comes Billy and Ben. If you tell them I'll thrash you."

Peter nodded.

The lack of practice showed in both the Invincibles' drilling and target shooting. The rest of the afternoon passed quickly. Tom kept an eye and an ear on Peter, but as far as Tom could tell, the Invincibles' sergeant said little more than a few words to anyone, and none of the boys came to question him about his leaving. When the time came for everyone to go home, Tom picked a day for another meeting, if the weather was good, and dismissed the company. He watched the boys leave one by one or in pairs until only Jake, Peter, and he remained. Jake said his goodbyes and stared off along the path by the creek. Tom whispered to Peter, "You promise not to tell?"

"I promise not to tell anyone your secret."

Convinced, Tom took off toward home. Had he looked back, he would have seen Peter running after Jake.

Worried that either Jake or Peter might accidentally reveal his plan, Tom decided that the sooner he left the better. He slowly began to gather supplies in an old sack that he hid under the loose board in the barn - an extra shirt; a pair of pants; socks; a blanket. He knew his mother would eventually miss them, but he planned to be on his way before she did. Food became his biggest problem. He figured he could carry a little when he started, enough for two or three days, but he could not risk taking too much as it might spoil. After he had eaten what he carried, he planned to stop at farms along the way and do some chores to earn meals. With nine days remaining in March, Tom picked the last Saturday of the month as the day he would leave. He would go out to do his chores right after eating a big breakfast and take a lunch with him, telling his mother that he had plans for the afternoon. Then he'd strike out along the road to Shimpstown. He didn't plan on letting anyone see him so that he could not be followed and found. If he had to, he would go across country, but always working his way south until he hit the Potomac River. After that he wasn't sure what he would do.

Tom's final, at least he thought it would be his final, meeting with the Invincibles took place exactly one week before he planned to leave. Nothing unusual happened, except that Johnny Myers accidently shot Ben Rankin on his backside when he lost his grip on the leather patch of his slingshot as he was drawing it to fire at the old tree. Ben leaped around and yelled at the top of his lungs while all the other boys writhed on the ground laughing at him. This time Tom stayed until everyone had left, or so he thought. As he watched Ben limp away and turned to go, two boys stepped from behind some bushes down near the creek. Tom recognized Jake and Peter.

"What are you two hangin' 'round for?" asked Tom suspiciously.

"We've been talkin'," answered Jake.

"'Bout what?"

"You runnin' away to join the army."

"You both promised not to tell nobody 'bout . . ."

"We didn't," argued Peter. "We both knew 'bout it, so Jake didn't have to tell me, and I didn't have to tell him."

"Well, what do you want?"

"We want to go with you."

Tom had expected Jake and Peter to try to talk him out of going or threaten to tell his mother. The idea that they would want to come with him had never entered his head.

"If we don't go with you . . . you ain't goin' nowhere. We'll tell your ma."

The old Tom would have started thrashing at that moment, but that Tom didn't exist anymore. This new Tom stood quietly for several long minutes, thinking. He had not wanted to admit it to himself, but he had been a little frightened about traveling alone through places he had never seen before and meeting people he would not know if he could trust. Having friends with him would make the journey that much more bearable. Still, he had to try and make them understand what their running away meant. He owed them that.

"I'd sure like to have both of you go with me, but what about your families? Won't they miss you as much as my mother'll miss me? Won't you miss them?"

"Our families are bigger than yours," argued Jake. "We have older brothers and sisters to do the work we do. Besides, we're tired of all the work. This is our chance to be real soldiers."

"We'll only be drummer boys."

"Drummer boys are soldiers. They just drum instead of shoot."

Nothing Tom could say changed Jake's and Peter's minds, so he explained what they would need to bring. When they parted, their plans were set. They would meet at the old tree early on Saturday morning. They decided that during the week they had left, each of them would try and find out about the roads leading south from Shimpstown. Of course, they could not ask anyone directly, but if they hung around the stores in town where people talked, they might learn something. Other than that, all they could do was wait and gather supplies.

During that final week Tom worked extra hard on the farm, getting as much done as he possibly could so that his mother would not have to hire anybody to do the little things and could save her money for the spring planting. Exhausted, he slept soundly every night. Then two days before he was to leave, a letter arrived from his father that convinced him he was doing the right thing. His mother read it after supper. It said.

> My dearest family,
>
> I seat myself down inside my tent that shelters me poorly from the pouring rain to write to you and tell you I am well. I had a brief spell of the fever last week and could hardly stand to do my picket duty. I am better now but ache at times in my bones. Jeremiah had it worse and went to hospital. I visited him when I could. He is growing stronger and will be back with me tomorrow.
>
> Our army sits here staring across the Rappahannock River at the enemy. Our great loss in the battle at Fredericksburg deeply saddened the men. We all felt it was for nothing and everyone lost faith in General Burnside. Our new commander,

General Hooker, has brought great change to the army. The men feel he can beat Bobby Lee and end this cruel war once the weather is good for marching.

I enclose some of my and Jeremiah's pay for you to use for the farm. Jeremiah and I can get along with very little as we do not have anything to spend our money on. The sutlers - traveling store keepers - swindle us at every turn and we do not gamble as many of the other men do. Jeremiah says that we can pay him back after the war by giving him a place to live and feed him.

It is soon my time to stand guard at the colonel's tent and I must end this letter. How I miss you all so terribly. I wish with all my heart that I could see you for just a few moments. I never thought being away from all of you would grieve me so deeply. As long as I am busy I am more at ease, but when I am alone in my tent or standing guard away from the men of my company, I am plunged into the deepest despair. This war is crueler than anything I could have imagined, for it tears loved ones apart. I kiss you all.

Your loving father and husband,
Jonathan

Both Tom and his mother cried. Ruth hugged her doll tightly while looking at her father's tintype. Rebecca finally stood up and began to gather up the dishes. Ruth, after tucking the tintype into her doll's apron, helped her. Tom left the house to bed down the horses for the night. If he had held any doubts about joining his father in the army, the letter had erased them all. His father needed him. His mother had Ruth; his father had no one. The letter proved that everything Tom had thought about running away and joining his father in the army had been true and right. Any doubts he may have had melted away with the words, "I miss you all so terribly."

The day before he was to leave, Tom hid the last of his supplies under the board in the barn. He wondered if Jake and Peter were doing the same thing in some secret hiding place he was sure that each of them had. Sitting for a few minutes before feeding the chickens one final time, he reviewed all his plans. He had learned very little about the roads south and hoped that Jake and Peter had done better. Though he felt anxious, he didn't feel afraid. The only thing he worried about was getting caught. He determined he would do whatever he had to do to make sure that did not happen. After a quick check under the board he grabbed the feed bucket and left the barn.

Saturday morning finally arrived, and after having a very good night's sleep – he had actually gone to bed early, giving the excuse that he had some hard work to do the next day – Tom sat at the table and ate until he could hold no more. He received some strange looks from his mother, but she kept filling his plate until he waved away her last stack of griddlecakes. These, along with some biscuits and some cold bacon, he wrapped in paper and stuffed into what had been a small flour sack.

"Where are you taking that?" his mother asked, her brow wrinkled with curiosity.

"I have some work to do that will take all day. I didn't want to come back for dinner so I thought I'd do what Pa did and take some food with me."

90

"My, you have become quite the hard-working boy lately. Perhaps you should take the day to play with your friends. The work can wait until Monday."

After a moment's panic, Tom responded, "Naw, I'd like to get this started so I can finish it as soon as I can."

"Well, all right, but you remember you're only a boy. Don't try to do a man's day's work."

Tom left quickly, not even hugging or kissing his mother. He didn't do that on other days when he went out to do the farm work, and he was afraid she would be suspicious if he did it today. He wanted to though, knowing it would be a long time before he saw her again. A few steps away from the porch, he stopped and turned around. Ruth stood on the bottom porch step, holding her doll and her father's tintype, as she always seemed to be doing. Tom started for the barn again, but heard Ruth following him. Again he turned. Ruth walked up to him and motioned for him to bend down. She whispered, "Goodbye."

CHAPTER 6

Runaways

The chill that ran up and down Tom's back did not come from the crisp March morning air he ran through as he dashed out the rear door of the barn and across the field toward the old tree down by the creek. It came from Ruth. Somehow she knew he was leaving – and not just for the day. Her "goodbye" had a tinge of sadness in it, but her smile was all joy, as if she understood something he did not. Even more disturbing, down deep inside him, he felt that she would not give him away, that she accepted the fact that he must go. Another wave of goose bumps popped out all over him. Would he ever become used to his sister's strange ways? He doubted it. And just in case his own gut-instinct about her not telling on him proved wrong, he ran faster.

A weary looking Peter sat slumped against the trunk of the old oak as Tom approached, somewhat out of breath. At almost the same moment Jake appeared along the path by the creek. Both dropped down by Peter. Only the sounds of the rippling water and the morning birds singing their lungs out broke the silence. Finally Peter spoke up, "I had a hard time getting away this morning. I thought I'd be late and miss you."

"How long you been here?" asked Jake.

"'Bout an hour."

"An hour! The sun wasn't even up yet!"

"Well . . ."

"It's all right, Peter," comforted Tom, knowing exactly how his sergeant felt.

"So what's the plan?" inquired Jake.

"I thought we'd go east of the seminary, cut through the cemetery, and go down the Shimpstown road."

"We goin' through Shimpstown?"

"Nah. I don't think we should let anyone see us 'til we're pretty far from here. I figure we can go west around Shimpstown."

"Then what?"

"I don't know. Just keep goin' south, I guess."

"Well, I found out that the road south from Shimpstown goes to Claylick and then goes east of the mountains to a place called Clear Spring. That's in Maryland. It's 'bout fifteen miles. I heard a man outside Brewer's store talkin' 'bout travelin' down there to see his cousin."

"How far is the Potomac River from Clear Spring?"

"He didn't say anything 'bout that, but it can't be that far. Can it?"

"Can't we get started," complained Peter. "I'd feel a whole lot better if we was walkin' instead of sittin'. I'm feelin' kinda sickly."

Both Tom and Jake admitted they were not feeling so well themselves; a case of nervous shakes, they decided. After a quick check in their sacks of extra clothing and other supplies, including their slingshots, to make sure each of them had what was needed for the journey, they struck out upstream until they could see the rear of the seminary. A quick dash across the road, and they melted into the woods. Keeping just inside the first line of trees, they made their way behind the seminary. Jake was the first to spot cemetery, making Tom feel much better - at least the first part of his plan had worked out successfully. Darting among the tombstones, Tom led the way toward the Shimpstown road. The three crowded behind a rather large monument to wait as a farmer drove his loaded wagon toward Mercersburg.

"I hope we don't run into many of them," whispered Tom.

"Why?" Peter wondered aloud.

"'Cause when our parents miss us tonight, they'll tell Constable Wolfe Sunday mornin'. Then he'll start searchin' for us. We got to be in Maryland before dark tonight without anyone seein' us. That way everyone will have to keep searchin' in all directions 'cause they won't know which way we went. If someone sees us they'll tell, and we'll get caught."

"We goin' to stay off the road then?"

"Can't. It would slow us down too much."

"We're goin' to have to stay right along the edge of the road and keep watchin' and listenin'. If we see or hear anythin', we'll dive into the brush."

"What if there ain't no brush?"

"Then we'll just have to hide the best we can. Now let's get started. We've got a long way to go."

Full stomachs, Peter's short legs, and a large dose of fear slowed the boys' progress to the point that it took them two hours to reach the outskirts of Shimpstown, which lay not quite a mile from Mercersburg. At every unusual sound and every flash of movement in the distance, Tom, Jake, and Peter dived for cover. Only once was it really necessary, when another farmer drove his wagon onto the road, this time going south. Lying in a thorn patch where he fell, Tom had had enough. "We'll never get to the river this way!" he growled. "The morning's half over, and we ain't got nowhere!"

"So what're we goin' to do?" Jake asked angrily, showing his own

95

frustration.

"We'll go around the town and get back on the road on the other side."

"We were goin' to do that anyway. I mean what're we goin' to do 'bout goin' so slow?"

"I been thinkin'," Peter interrupted. "We didn't really see nobody but that there farmer since we left the cemetery, and we spotted him when he was pretty far off. He couldn't've seen us or if he did he couldn't've made us out exactly. We've been jumpin' like frogs on a fryin' pan. Maybe we should just walk right down the road and only take cover when we think somebody might see us."

"I thought that's what we were doin'," complained Jake.

"No, Peter's right," observed Tom. "We've been divin' into the brush at every little thing. If we're goin' to get anywhere we're goin' to have to move faster and that means we got to take some chances. Even if some farmer sees us from far off, he won't know exactly what he saw and by that time we'll have seen him and can hide."

Satisfied with the new strategy, Tom guided his small column around Shimpstown. It wasn't much of a "town" at all, just a few houses clumped together along the road. A few people were spotted doing morning chores, but they were too busy to notice three boys darting between the trees. Tom had excellent sense of direction, something he had inherited from his father, but he now stood on a road that ran east and west. It wasn't what he had expected. "I don't think this is the right road," he confessed, more to himself that to Jake and Peter, but they heard him.

"You got us lost already?" teased Jake.

"Nah."

"So which way do we go?"

"Look over there. It's a creek. It's flowin' east. If we follow that it'll

96

lead us to the road we want.'

"Now how do you know that?"

"We know the road to Claylick runs south from Shimpstown, so if this here creek keeps runnin' east it has to cross that road. Besides, if we go along the creek, we can't be seen like we could if we go along the road."

Jake had to admit that Tom's plan made sense, so he agreed. Everything was as Tom said it would be for a few hundred yards. Then the stream took a sharp turn south. Tom noticed it right away but said nothing, hoping that the creek would still run into the road before Jake or Peter noticed the change. Gradually it began to shift toward the southeast, allowing Tom to breathe more easily. By the time the run entered a patch of woods, it had once more shifted almost due east. Tom relaxed and, walking on, suddenly came out of the trees directly onto the road. Triumphantly he turned to Jake, who was right behind him, and bragged, "I told you that I knew where . . ." His words caught in his throat when he saw the look on Jake's face. Peter, staring over Jake's left shoulder wore the same shocked appearance. It took Tom several seconds to understand, and when he did, he spun around to see a man sitting on a horse that was taking a drink from the stream as it meandered over the road.

"You boys look like you seen some sort of ghost," the stranger said with some amusement. Unable to utter a single word, Tom stood, anchored to the spot. The man continued, "I just come through Claylick. I'm headin' to Mercersburg. You boys know anything about the place." Still unable to speak, all three shrugged in unison. "You boys ain't much for conversation, are you?" Three heads shook. "You ever been to Mercersburg?" Open-mouthed stares answered the question. "I 'spect not. Guess you don't even know how far I got to go either." Three shrugs. "Didn't think so. I come up through Clear

Spring. That's in Maryland. Nice ride. My horse decided he was thirsty. I was hopin' to make Mercersburg by noon." Blank faces. "Well, thanks for your help, such as it were. I got to be on my way." And finally, the man rode off.

"What'll we do now?" Peter mumbled, the first one of the three to regain the power of speech.

"I swear, I didn't see him," pleaded Tom.

"Neither did we," confessed Jake. "It don't matter no how. He saw us, and he's goin' to Mercersburg. Tomorrow when they find out we're missin' someone's sure to ask if anybody saw three boys along any of the roads comin' into town. They'll be chasin' after us pretty quick then."

"Maybe not."

"How you figure that?"

"Before they can ask him they got to find him. If he's visitin' someone he may not hear about us bein' gone at all."

"You know how fast news goes through town. If a chicken laid a square egg at one end of town people would know it at the other end five minutes later."

"You think he's got a chicken that lays square eggs?" asked Peter, looking completely confused. "I didn't see no chicken."

Tom rolled his eyes but held his temper. "All I'm sayin' is that somebody would have to tell Constable Wolfe that a stranger was in town. Then Constable Wolfe would have to find him and ask him. That could take half the day if Constable Wolfe was out lookin' for us in every which direction."

"Do you think square eggs'd taste the same as regular eggs?"

"Forget the square eggs!" yelled Tom, giving in to his anger at last.

"I was just wonderin'."

"Can't do anythin' 'bout it now. We got to move on and fast."

Having somewhat recovered from the fright they received at meeting the horseman, the three boys stepped onto the road, and got another. The village of Claylick loomed just a few hundred yards away from where they stood. The stream had taken them farther south than Tom had realized. A wagon coming toward them at a snail's pace sent them back into the woods where they huddled until it passed. Sticking to the cover of the brush and trees, they made their way cautiously around the houses and barns. A few gut-wrenching dashes across open ground pushed them to the breaking point. Tom called a halt in a small hollow just off the road about a quarter of a mile south of the last house.

"We'll rest here and eat," he ordered, his place as commander of the Invincibles taking over.

Neither Jake nor Peter argued with him. They all sat quietly gnawing away at a cold dinner and drinking water from corked bottles. As he bit into a cold griddlecake, Tom tried to focus on what lay ahead, but he could not get the horseman and the consequences of meeting him out of his mind. Once the man told his story, a few men on good horses could cover the five or six miles between Mercersburg and Claylick in no time. The question came down to when Constable Wolfe would find out which way they had gone, and even though he had tried to sound confident, Tom knew Jake had been right about the square egg. The news about the man meeting three boys near Claylick would spread fast. Tom looked back over his shoulder toward the village. A road branched out from it toward the west. He reasoned that it must connect with the road through Blair's Valley - the same road that the Rebels had used to reach Mercersburg. As he ate the last bit of griddlecake he made up his mind. "We're goin' back to that road and go west."

"Go west?" blurted out Jake in surprise, sending a chunk of

biscuit flying through the air. "How's goin' west goin' to get us to the river if it's south?"

"If that there horseman does tell Constable Wolfe 'bout us, he'll come a howlin' down this here road like a scalded cat, and he'll catch us too. He'll have every man with a horse out lookin' for us. We'll run out of food and water and then he'll get us."

"Say he would. How does goin' west keep him off us?"

"He'll think we're on this road, and he won't search the road through Blair's Valley. Nobody's seen us on that road and if we're careful, nobody will. Even if some people do see us, it won't matter 'cause they'll have nobody to tell with everyone tryin' to find us on this here road."

The two faces looking at him began to smile. Heads nodded and suddenly laughter filled the air. Tom had to remind both his friends, "Quiet. We still don't want anybody to see us if we can help it."

The trek to the Blair's Valley road consumed the rest of the day. The boys wanted to make absolutely sure nobody saw so much as a single hair of any of them. That way, if Constable Wolfe checked along the road, no one would be able to tell him a thing. Hopefully he wouldn't check, but if he did, he'd get nothing but shrugs and shaking heads for answers to his questions. Unfortunately, the tension caused by the need to be constantly alert took its toll. By the time the boys came in view of the Blair's Valley road the sun was setting and their strength all but gone.

"We need to find someplace to stay the night," whimpered Peter. "I'm done in and my feet hurt up to my knees."

"How about that mill over there?" offered Tom. "Won't have nobody in it during the night and we can be up and gone before anybody comes in the morning."

"I'm for that," Jake groaned, rubbing his own aching feet.

Huddling behind a line of bushes that ran along a split rail fence, Tom, Jake, and Peter watched in the growing twilight until they were certain that the mill was empty. Even then they didn't rush forward and inside its welcoming walls. Tom insisted that he go first and check to make sure that no one was there. Jake and Peter watched Tom worm his way along the fence and then dart across the road and over the creek – the mill being on the opposite side. His going failed to disturb the stillness of the approaching night. Tom disappeared into the shadow of the mill. Fearing that they would not be able to see Tom's signal, Jake and Peter, still behind the fence, moved down the road to a better vantage point. For a few minutes they saw nothing. Then a figure stepped out of the shadows and waved. Checking the road carefully to make sure all was clear, Jake and Peter bolted for the mill.

The placid sounds of rippling water enveloped the boys as they made themselves as comfortable as possible in a corner of the mill next to a window. The cloudless sky permitted the starlight to fall through the opening, bathing the boys in its ghostly glow. They ate ravenously, their stomachs growling. When finished they arranged some empty grain sacks into soft piles and collapsed on them. "You think we ought to take turns stayin' awake?" Peter asked. "What if somebody comes in or we don't get up early enough?"

"Never heard of anybody grindin' grain at night," responded Tom, "and one of us is bound to be up early enough to wake the others before somebody comes."

Peter didn't argue, and Jake was already asleep. Tom rolled over. He tried to plan for tomorrow, but his body's weariness claimed him and he drifted off. He slept fitfully at first, his leg muscles and feet aching, but soon he fell into a deep slumber.

Voices jerked Tom awake. A quick glance told him that Jake and

Peter still slept soundly. Once his senses fully returned, he determined that the two men who were talking stood just outside the window above his head. Quietly, he crawled over to Jake and, placing a hand over his friend's mouth, shook him awake. A bit groggy at first, Jake understood the situation as soon as he heard the voices. He turned over and awoke Peter. Forgetting to put his hand over Peter's mouth nearly revealed their presence as Peter blurted out, "What happened!" Fortunately the discussion the two men were having had turned into a loud argument, and they didn't hear him. Tom and Jake both shushed Peter before he could say another word.

Gathering up their things and restacking the sacks as they had found them, the boys looked around for a way out. The door they had entered was still closed, but the men stood too near it. Jake pointed to a ladder that passed both up through an opening in the floor above and down through a similar hole in the floor they stood on. Up would not be a wise choice, and scrambling for the ladder, they climbed downward. The large gears and shafts that turned the millstone on the floor above filled a good part of the room they dropped into. Once more, eyes searched for an escape route. Peter elbowed Tom and pointed to a small door on the south side of the room. A creak coming from above them, followed by footsteps, told them that the men had entered the mill. Picking their way gingerly around the mill's mechanism, some barrels, and several piles of grain sacks, they reached the door. Lifting the door's latch, Tom gave it a gentle pull. It didn't budge an inch. He grabbed the latch with both hands and pulled harder. Still it would not move. Motioning for Jake to help him, the two heaved together. With a loud creak the door gave way and opened a few inches. The sound turned them to stone, but almost immediately the gears behind them started turning and making their own grinding and groaning sounds. With a sigh of relief, Tom and

Jake attacked the stubborn door once more, and in seconds had it standing open far enough for them to squeeze through.

"So much for gettin' an early start," mocked Jake.

"Who woke who?" Tom growled back.

"How we goin' to get away without bein' seen?" asked Peter, bringing the budding argument to an abrupt end. "There's a house right over there."

"The creek," pointed Tom.

"Yeah, but which way?"

"Can't risk crossin' the road so we'll go west, upstream."

The boys hugged the south wall of the mill, slowly working their way to the southwest corner of the building. From there they hoped to reach the stream and follow it west away from the road. The shock they received when they came to the corner of the mill wrecked that plan immediately. The mill stood in the fork of two roads. In the dark of the night before, none of them had noticed the second one. Either way they went they would have to cross a road and lose the cover of the stream's banks.

"Now what?" demanded Jake.

"Nothin' to do," answered Tom, "but make a run for it."

"Yeah, but which way?"

Tom pointed west.

"Wait," called Peter in a voice just above a whisper.

"What now," snarled Tom.

"There's a lady on the porch of that house."

Sure enough, a lady stood at the end of the porch of the house across the road north of the mill. It took but a moment for Tom to grasp what she was doing, having done the same thing many times. She was scattering chicken feed. "She's feedin' the chickens, but she's lookin' this way. We'll have to wait."

Suddenly, Jake gave Tom's shirt a yank. "Look yonder," he moaned.

A wagon came rumbling up the Blair's Valley road directly toward them. Still too far away for the driver to see them clearly, it would not be long before he would. Tom glanced back at the lady on the porch in time to see her set the feed bucket down and walk down the steps. As soon as she disappeared around the corner of the house, he motioned to Jake and Peter to follow him and raced across the open ground. He ran at his top speed over the road and into the bushes that lined the banks of the creek, not bothering to look back. The pounding of two pairs of feet assured him that Jake and Peter were right on his heels. Once under cover, he slumped down, his back braced against a small maple tree. He had not run that far, but the combination of his fear at being seen and his mad dash caused him to take in rapid gulps of air. Jake and Peter joined him, their own lungs heaving mightily.

"That was close," Peter managed to say at last.

"I should've listened to you last night," admitted Tom. "We should've taken turns stayin' awake and keepin' watch. If somebody would've seen us . . ."

"I don't think any of us could've stayed awake," declared Jake. I know I couldn't't've.

"Think anybody saw us?" asked Peter.

"Nobody yelled," said Tom with a sigh of relief, "so I guess we got away clean."

"How far we goin' to follow this here creek?" questioned Peter.

"'Til we can find a place to turn south that's out of sight."

"Well, before we start lookin', can we eat?"

"That's what I was goin' to say next."

Breakfast didn't take too long. Neither did the realization that they had eaten far too much of their food the day before. Tom had planned to have enough to last for at least two days, and he had hoped for three. Except for a bit of jerky and one biscuit, his food sack was empty. Jake's and Peter's were equally bare. Their next meal would have to be scrounged, meaning either worked for or stolen. Neither of those choices pleased him. By the looks on their faces, Jake and Peter understood his thoughts exactly.

Following the stream west for scarcely two hundred yards, the boys found a much smaller creek flowing from the south into it. The little run wound its way through a small patch of woods, and Tom decided to take the chance and see where it led. After about a quarter of a mile it came to a road that ran east and west. Looking east, Tom could see the mill in the distance. Gazing southeast he could make out the Blair's Valley road. A house stood across the road, but no one seemed to be about. He dropped down on his haunches and explained; "I think we can get back to the Blair's Valley road by cutting across the fields over there."

"Most of that's right out in the open," observed Jake.

"We've already lost half the mornin'. We got to get movin'. Either of you got a better plan?"

Jake shrugged. Peter shook his head. Tom stood up and darted across the road into a farm lane. The lane was lined on both sides with fences, giving them some cover. Tom decided to stay on it as long as it went in the right direction. They ran. Coming to a fork in the lane, just past a house that looked abandoned, Tom turned east toward the Blair's Valley road. His luck held as this lane took them exactly where he wanted to go. Peeking around the fence corner, looking south – Jake did the same, looking north – Tom could see nothing but clear road. Jake shook his tousled head, indicating a clear road. The next minute three rather dirty, disheveled boys sauntered along the road as if they had not a care in the world, though inside each one wondered what lay ahead.

The afternoon passed without any major confrontations with travelers. Three times the boys had to hide off the road to let someone pass. Farmers were seen in their fields, but most were too far away to see them and the ones that were closer paid them no mind. With the day waning, Tom's stomach started reminding him that it needed to be fed. He chewed on his last piece of jerky and biscuit, Jake and Peter doing the same with the bits of food they had left. The few morsels only made them hungrier. Tom's mind focused on how to get their next meal.

Directly ahead Tom could see that a mountain rose up, blocking the end of the valley. A gap appeared to its right and to its left. He also noticed that a road branched off to the right, passing through the western gap, while the main road continued on through the eastern gap. Jake saw it too and asked, "Which way do we go?"

"We'll worry about that after we get somethin' to eat and find a place to sleep," Tom replied.

"There's still plenty of light. We could go on for awhile."

"We could, but we got to eat, and there's only two ways of doin' it. We can try to steal somethin' or we can work for a meal. By the time we do one or the other, it'll be dark. As for me, I vote to work for it."

"Where we goin' to find work?" asked Peter.

"Maybe at one of the farms here 'bout."

"But then we'll be seen."

"I know, but do you want to go without eatin'?"

"No."

"Then let's try that farm right there."

Three farms later, stomachs still empty, the boys stopped at the end of a farm lane. Tom and Peter flopped on their backs in some tall grass. Jake climbed a nearby fence. Discouraged, tired, and miserable, Tom sat wondering what to do next.

"There's still a few farms ahead," called Jake from his roost atop the rail fence. "We might as well try them. There's still enough light to work by."

Tom dragged himself to his feet and trudged off after Jake, wondering where his lieutenant got all his energy. Peter moped along beside Tom. Reaching the lane, Jake suggested that he talk to the farmer. Tom had no complaints and leaned against a fence post as Jake walked up to the door of the house. He knocked and a woman answered. Neither Tom nor Peter could hear what Jake told her, but the next thing they knew Jake was waving them to join him.

The woman, a Mrs. Thompson, quickly assigned the boys various chores and sent them off, telling them she would cook them a meal while they worked. Tom wanted badly to ask Jake what he had said but soon was so busy he didn't have time. Mrs. Thompson came out and lit some lamps in the barn so the boys could see to work. It was well after dark when they completed their tasks. Jake went to the house and told Mrs. Thompson that they had finished and that she could come out and check on what they had done. She seemed very satisfied and told the boys where to wash up before coming in for supper.

Not a morsel of food remained on any of the plates that Mrs. Thompson set on her table that night. She seemed to glow as she watched the boys devour her stew and bread. By the time he had licked the last bit of gravy from his plate, Tom thought he may not be able to stand, so full was his stomach. Jake and Peter looked equally stuffed. Mrs. Thompson chuckled, "My, my. You boys certainly know how to do a meal justice. Makes me feel all giddy to see you eat like that. My dear departed husband and our two sons used to eat in the same fashion. Both my boys are off servin' in the army. God keep them safe so they can come home to me. Now the three of you can

107

sleep in the barn and in the morning, I have a few more chores that need doin'. I'll make you a fine breakfast as payment. That sound all right with you?"

Tom, Jake, and Peter all shook their heads.

"I've set some blankets on the chair by the door. Just remember to bring them in with you in the morning. Now off with you. I have dishes to wash."

"She didn't even ask who we were, where we're from, or where we're goin'," marveled Peter, as the three trudged toward the barn.

"I was wonderin' 'bout that too," confessed Jake. "What do you make of it, Tom?"

"She still might ask tomorrow. Let me do the talkin' if she does."

"Fine with me."

"Me too," echoed Peter.

But Mrs. Thompson didn't ask and Tom didn't offer any explanation. He, Jake, and Peter did the chores that Mrs. Thompson asked them to do and then sat down to a breakfast fit for kings. Bacon, biscuits, jam, griddlecakes, maple syrup, eggs, and cold spring water disappeared into hungry mouths as fast as Mrs. Thompson could put them on the table. Even after the boys could not cram another bite down into their stomachs, she continued to cook away at her stove. When finished she set three small sacks of food on the table, saying, "That should help you get along to wherever it is that you're goin'. The three of you be careful. It's an unforgivin' world we're livin' in these days. Thank you for all your help. Now be off with you before I get too attached."

"Could you tell us the way to Clear Spring, please?" Tom asked, as he stood in the doorway.

Without looking up from the table she was clearing, Mrs. Thompson answered, "Take the road at the end of the lane south until it ends. Take the right fork. It'll take you right into Clear Spring."

"Thank you."

The boys reached the end of the short farm lane and as one turned around. Mrs. Thompson stood framed in her doorway. She raised one arm and then quickly stepped back inside and closed the door.

"I really liked her," muttered Peter.

"Me, too," mumbled Jake.

"We all did," admitted Tom, and after a long pause to swallow the lump in his throat, he added, "Now let's start walking. We must get to the river before night."

CHAPTER 7

River Raiders

C lear Spring reminded the boys of Mercersburg, causing a wave of homesickness that Tom nipped in the bud by suggesting they find out the quickest way to the Potomac River. A friendly blacksmith, pounding away at a wagon wheel rim in front of his shop on the outskirts of the town, pointed down the road that led straight through the center of Clear Spring, all the while ogling the boys with a curious look that Tom didn't like one little bit. His question answered, Tom moved quickly, not wanting to give the man any time to ask his own questions, and started off down the road, calling back over his shoulder to Jake and Peter to get them moving as well. They trudged after him.

Tom was not very happy about having to pass through the center of the town. If word about their running away had somehow beaten them to Clear Spring, people might be on the lookout for three boys walking together. He decided it was time to split up and ordered Jake to one side of the street and Peter to the other. He would hang back and cross back and forth from one side to the other as they made their way through town. Hopefully, no one would notice three strange boys walking separately. They didn't. Along the way, Tom got up enough nerve to ask a passerby how to get to the river.

"Depends on what you want to do when you get there," the

111

stranger replied. "If you want to catch a boat on the canal, I'd go to Four Locks. The boats slow down there quite a bit. If you just want to see the river . . ."

"I'd like to go to Four Locks," Tom interrupted, thinking it better to let the stranger think he was trying to catch a canal boat.

Once he had the directions, Tom moved on rapidly, catching up with Jake and Peter at the southern edge of town.

"Where were you?" asked Peter anxiously. "We thought somebody caught you."

"I stopped to ask a man the best way to get to the river. We're headin' for a place called Four Locks."

"Is it a big place?"

"It ain't no place at all," grumbled Jake. "Don't you two know nothin' 'bout canals?"

"Never needed to know nothin' 'bout them," growled Peter, somewhat embarrassed.

"Well, canals have locks, kind of like big troughs, that a boat goes into. It's closed at one end and when the boat gets in, they close it at the other."

"Why?" questioned Peter.

Jake had used up his entire knowledge of canals and canal boats in his short tirade, so he just cuffed Peter on the arm and complained, "We ain't got time to stand around, talkin' 'bout somethin' you'll see for yourself soon. Right Tom?"

Tom could see that Jake had bitten off more than he could chew and ended the argument with, "Come on. We still got a ways to go."

Late in the afternoon, Tom topped a small rise of ground and came to a sudden halt. Jake and Peter, a few steps behind asked simultaneously, "What's wro . . .?" Their question died on their lips as they came up beside Tom and stared with him at the biggest river

112

any of them had ever seen.

"Sure is big!" marveled Peter. "You know I can't swim none too good."

"How we goin' to cross it?" Jake asked, his voice filled with awe and a bit of fear.

"Maybe there's a bridge," offered Tom.

"Don't see none."

"I told you I don't swim so good, didn't I," repeated Peter.

"Maybe we can take a boat," suggested Tom, hopefully.

"Yeah, one of them there canal boats."

"Canal boats don't go on rivers," explained Jake. "They go on canals. Look over there. See that little river that runs alongside the big river. That's the canal. The canal boats go on the little river, not the big one."

"Don't make any sense to me. Besides, I ain't never heard of two rivers runnin' side by side before."

Frustrated, Jake growled at Tom, "Can't we get goin' instead of standin' here. You two ain't never goin' to understand 'til you see it for youselfs."

Even standing next to the canal, Peter could not take his eyes off the river that stretched out before him, looking so much wider than it had from the hill. Jake pointed to a canal boat and a lock, but Peter didn't appear to notice. Tom watched as a boat entered a lock and went through the process of being lowered to the next level of the water. In the fading light, he could also see that Jake had been wrong about one thing. Four Locks was a place – of sorts. Several buildings lined a road that ran alongside the canal. A few were houses and the rest looked like barns or warehouses, like those he had seen in Chambersburg on one of the three trips he had taken there with his father. "That's where we'll spend the night," he declared, pointing to the nearest barnlike structure. "We'll wait here 'til it gets dark and then find a way in."

As they waited, they ate some of the food in their sacks, each of them quietly thanking Mrs. Thompson for her cooking skills and her generosity. Once darkness had fallen, Tom led the way to the barn. He had no trouble finding a way in – a side door that had a lock that wasn't fastened. The interior was pitch black and for a moment Tom opened the door wide to let in some moonlight. In the dimness, he could see piles of grain sacks – not the most comfortable of beds but good enough for one night. In fact, it mattered little. Had the sacks been filled with rocks, the boys would have slept just as soundly.

A loud creaking noise jolted Tom from his slumber. Coming quickly to his senses, he growled at himself for oversleeping again. A bright light flooded into the gloomy interior of the barn. It took a few moments for Tom to realize that the large doors at the front of the barn had been opened. Jake and Peter, awakened as well, rolled off their sack-beds and joined Tom on the floor where he had dropped. Slowly they wormed their way to the side door. Tom sneaked a peek over the stacks of grain sacks and saw several men grabbing sacks and lugging them outside the barn to a waiting wagon. While the men's backs were turned, the boys slipped out the door and darted to the nearby cover of some bushes.

"That was close," whispered Tom.

"Too close," replied Jake. "What now, Captain?"

"Let's eat. I'll think better after."

As he chewed, Tom created and discarded several plans until at last he conjured one that made some sense – at least to him. Since none of them really knew anything about the river or the canal, including Jake, Tom reasoned that they would need someone who did to help them. That someone had to be a person who knew all about the canal and the river. Such a person could tell them where they could cross the river, and help them find the best way of reaching wherever that was. So concentrated was Tom on his planning that he didn't notice Peter, who barely touched his food. Jake, chewing away as if he hadn't had food in a month, didn't notice either. Finally, having had his fill, Tom looked into his sack and smiled. There was still enough for one more meal. He tied the sack shut and lifted his eyes to see how Peter and Jake fared. Only then did he see the terrified look on Peter's face.

"What's wrong with you?" Tom asked.

"I hardly slept last night, and I can't eat," answered Peter.

"Why?"

"I can't go with you . . . across the river. I'm too scared. I'm goin' home. I'm sorry, Tom, but when I saw that river, how wide it was. I just got all cold inside."

"We ain't goin' to swim the river. You don't have to be scared of it."

"'Tain't 'bout swimmin'. I miss my Ma and family. Mrs. Thompson reminded me so much of my ma. She's at home worryin' 'bout me. I got to go home to her. It ain't right what I'm doin'. You're goin' to your Pa and that's good. I ain't got no reason to cross that river. I was wrong to come with you."

You can't back out now!" exclaimed Jake, his face reddening by the second. "We're Invincibles! Invincibles don't quit and go home!"

"Jake!" yelled Tom. "Come over here." Tom led Jake to a large tree and stepped partially behind it.

"You can't let him quit!" argued Jake. "You got to order him to go with us!"

"I can't do that, Jake. Besides he's right. Neither of you should

115

have come with me. I was wrong to tell you I was goin' and wrong in lettin' you come with me. I was scared to go alone. I ain't scared no more. I'll get to my pa. I know I will. But you got to take Peter home. He can't get there hisself."

"I ain't takin' him home. I'm stayin' with you."

"I'm still captain of the Invincibles. Ain't I?"

Jake paused for a long moment before dropping his eyes and answering, "Yeah."

"Then I order you to take Sergeant Bricker home, Lieutenant."

"That ain't fair and you know it!"

"You're the one who said we was still Invincibles. And you said I was still captain."

"Yeah, but . . ."

"Jake. You know you got to do this."

"Yeah, I know, but I ain't got to like doin' it, do I?"

Tom handed over his sack of food to Jake, figuring that he could get more somewhere along the canal. Peter looked even worse than he had before – the news that Jake would go with him only making him feel more embarrassed. Tom ordered both Jake and Peter to keep up the drilling of the Invincibles, telling them that he expected them to be even better when he got home. The "good-byes" were short. As Tom watched Jake and Peter disappear down the road a knot rose into his throat and his chest tightened. He had lied when he said he wasn't afraid to go on alone. He was. But he couldn't give up. His pa needed him. He turned on his heels and headed for the canal. He had to find out where to cross the river.

"Not like that, you scurvy excuse for a seaman!"

Tom had been standing next to one of the locks on the canal, watching a canal boat named *Decatur* slip into the lock. An old,

116

gray-bearded man, wearing a dark blue coat and hat splattered with gold braid, stood on the bow of the boat, yelling at a younger man on shore who was attempting to do something with a thick rope. "You there! Boy! Give that man a hand with that rope and be quick about it," cried the old man. It took Tom a few seconds to understand that the old man was yelling at him. At first he just ignored the order, but a second, "Well, boy. Give the man a hand!" jostled him into action. When finished, the canal boat was firmly tied in place.

"Thank you for your help. My man is good with cargo but a poor seaman with a rope. Can't tie a knot worth tyin'. We got to take on cargo here. Say, you look like a strong lad. Care to earn a dollar. If you can lift and carry 50-pound grain sacks, I could sure use the help. By the way, I'm Captain Michael Mulligan, late of the United States Navy. I was a powder monkey on the *USS Gurriere* under that great Captain of the Seas, Stephen Decatur, himself. Fought with him at Tripoli in the Second Barbary War, I did. Named this here boat after him, I did. Now, you want the job or no."

Tom stood, mouth agape, staring at the grizzled old veteran of a war Tom had never heard of, wondering what exactly a powder monkey was and if he should take the offer or not. The captain's glare seemed to bore holes right through him, causing considerable discomfort. To save himself further agony, Tom nodded.

"Good, boy. You just follow Seaman Pertwey and he'll show you what to do."

Tom was big for his age – strong too. He had helped his father at times with sacks as large and heavy as the ones he now carried from barn to wagon and from wagon to boat, but he had never carried so many in so short a time before. By the time the boat's hold was filled, he was completely exhausted. When Captain Mulligan handed him his well-earned dollar, Tom could barely lift his arm to take it.

"You look plum done in, boy," said Captain Mulligan, concernedly, "but you did a day's work any man could be proud of. Say, what's you name? I don't reckon you told me."

"My name is Tom."

"You live 'round here. I can't say I ever saw you hereabouts before and I've been up and down this here canal for nigh on to ten years."

Tom was too tired to think clearly, and before he knew it, he was telling Captain Mulligan his story. "I don't live here. I'm goin' down river to a place I can cross. I'm tryin' to get to my pa. He's in the army and . . ." Suddenly realizing what he was saying, Tom caught himself and said no more.

"So you run off to join your pa in the army."

Tom looked for a way out, but he was standing on the boat with Captain Mulligan between him and the shore. Exhausted and aching in every muscle, he sat down on a grain sack. "Yeah. My ma is back at home. She has my sister, Ruth. I wanted to join my pa so we could be together."

"Ran away from home to join the navy, I did. I know just what you're up against. What say you join my crew, and I'll take you down river where you can cross? I might even be able to help you get to your pa if he's with the army at Fredericksburg."

Not able to believe what he heard, Tom asked, "You mean you'll help me get to my pa?"

"That's what I said."

Overjoyed, Tom agreed. Captain Mulligan assigned Tom to the towrope to help with the mules that pulled the boat along the canal. Since it was near dark, however, Captain Mulligan decided to tie off the *Decatur* on the river side of the canal until morning.

He told Tom that he could sleep in the small cabin at the bow of the boat, but he must first join the captain and crew at one of the local establishments for a meal. Tom didn't argue, being as hungry as a bear. Everyone crossed the canal on one of the closed locks. Having his own money, Tom insisted that he pay for his own food. He splurged and spent thirty cents for a meal that filled him to the brim. On returning to the *Decatur*, Tom had no problem when Captain Mulligan suggested that he turn in early. Seconds after his head hit the bed, he was asleep.

Morning brought a flurry of activity. A hearty breakfast was immediately followed with preparations to get underway. The *Decatur* was drawn toward the towpath side of the canal and Tom leaped off and joined the man in charge of the two mules that provided the canal boat with its power. Tom tried hard to follow exactly what the man leading the first mule did, not wanting to disappoint Captain Mulligan.

The little village of Four Locks got its name because there were four locks - numbers 50, 49, 48, and 47 - right in a row at this place on the canal. The *Decatur* passed through them slowly. Captain Mulligan stood on the bow of his boat and yelled instructions - or just yelled - at every crewman, including Tom. Sam Radford, the man in charge of the mules, called back to Tom, "Never you mind the captain. He just enjoys yellin' at everybody and every thing. Makes him feel like he's back at sea. You'll know if he really gets mad at you. You'll end up in the canal."

Once through the fourth lock, the mules pulled the towrope taut and the *Decatur* made its way along the canal. The mules seemed to know exactly what to do so Tom just walked along beside his and took in the scenery. In a short while he began staring at the far side of the river whenever he could see it through the trees and undergrowth between the river and the canal. He felt the river was the last barrier between him and his father. Once across it, he thought he would be safe from anyone trying to find him to take him back to Mercersburg.

The day passed slowly. The steady pace of the mules, broken up only when the boat passed through locks, never wavered. Locks 46 and 45 were passed. A long stretch of canal brought the boat to Williamsport and Lock 44. Captain Mulligan did not stop at the town but kept on through Lock 44, and hours later through Lock 43. As the boat approached Locks 42 and 41, the sun stood on the mountaintops to the west, and Captain Mulligan decided to tie off the boat on the river side of the canal for the night. There would be no going out for a meal. Some of the crew lit a fire on shore and cooked a meal that all enjoyed. Again, Tom settled down in the bow cabin for the night, not knowing that he was not going to get much sleep.

Neither Captain Mulligan nor any of his crew suspected that the glow of their cooking fire had been seen from across the river by men who, while not dressed in gray, nevertheless fought for the Confederacy. Their job was to do anything they could to hurt the Union cause. That included damaging Union property or the property of citizens loyal to the United States. From the time the war had begun men like these had tried to interrupt canal boat traffic by damaging the canal, its locks, and its boats, as well as stealing the mules that drew the boats along the canal. On this very night, they planned a raid across the river, and Captain Mulligan's cooking fire had given them a target.

The sound of a shot startled Tom to consciousness. Flickering lights flashing through the small cabin windows above him formed dancing figures on the wall next to his bunk. It took but a moment or two for Tom to become fully awake to the sounds of shouting men and scuffling on the deck of the boat. Captain Mulligan's voice could be heard above everything. "Pirates! Pirates my lads! Prepare to repel boarders!" Another shot caused Tom to dive into the sack he had brought from home and grab his slingshot and a handful of lead bullets. Loading his slingshot, he scrambled out on the bow of the *Decatur* to see a sight he would never forget. There amidst the shining three-quarter moon, the glow of torches, and the fire that the crew had kept burning on shore, he saw men struggling on the deck of the boat and around the fire. Captain Mulligan had a crew of five men, including Tom. Two of them were wrestling with other men between the boat and the fire on shore. Two more struggled with two men at the stern of the boat. Captain Mulligan, a cutlass in his hand, stood on a pile of grain sacks covered with canvas in the middle of the boat, swinging at three men who were armed with what Tom thought were muskets.

"Give up old man!" called one of the raiders fighting Captain Mulligan. "Your boat's as good as burned and unless you give up you'll burn with it!"

Tom saw a fire toward the stern of the boat beyond where Captain Mulligan stood. A torch thrown by one of the pirates had lit a pile of empty grain sacks. Unless they were pitched overboard soon the boat would surely catch fire. At that instant, one of the raiders, standing nearest to Tom with one foot on the very edge of the boat and the other on the canvas covered grain sacks, raised his musket to fire at Captain Mulligan. Tom was quicker. He drew back his slingshot and fired. The lead bullet sped through the air, striking the raider on the side of the head and catapulting him off the boat and into the narrow slip of water between the boat and the shore. Tom reloaded and fired again at the next raider who had leaped up on top of the pile of grain sacks on one side of Captain Mulligan while his partner came at the captain from the other side.

Not having had time to take accurate aim, Tom's shot hit the man on his leg behind his right knee. With a howl, the raider dropped down and grasped his injured limb with one hand. A wild swipe of Captain Mulligan's cutlass sent the raider's musket flying from his other hand. Tom quickly reloaded his slingshot and taking careful aim fired past Captain Mulligan, hitting the other raider square in the chest. The impact of the lead bullet knocked him backward and caused him to drop his musket. Captain Mulligan, yelling strange oaths, turned and charged him. Meanwhile, Tom let loose a barrage of lead bullets at the raider with the wounded knee, striking him in the back. Weaponless, the raider swung around, only to catch a bullet right in the middle of his forehead. Dazed, he staggered to the edge of the boat and joined his fellow raider in the canal. Captain Mulligan soon sent his adversary racing for shore. Tom saw some of the raiders fighting on land, scurry over to the canal to help their injured and nearly drowned friends out of the water. Tom made them very uncomfortable by firing the last of his lead bullets at them, enjoying the yelps of those he managed to hit. The *Deactur*'s crew soon sent the rest of the raiders skedaddling back to their rowboats and the opposite side of the Potomac.

Once everyone had calmed down, Captain Mulligan took stock of his boat's losses. The crew escaped with some minor cuts and bruises, but the captain himself suffered more serious injuries. The first shot that Tom had heard had grazed the captain's head, and he had burned his hands when he threw the torch and burning grain sacks into the canal. Sam cleaned and dressed the captain's wounds. As he did he asked Captain Mulligan, "What made them take to running like they did? They outnumbered us aplenty. I thought we was done for and the boat lost for sure."

"Our youngest crew member there," Captain Mulligan replied, nodding his head toward Tom, "somehow turned the tables on them. One minute I was fightin' three of the scalawags and the next thing I knew two of them were bathin' in the canal, and the third staggerin' around gaspin' for air like somebody hit him in the chest with a sledge hammer. What did you do to them, Tom?"

Tom sheepishly held up his slingshot. The entire crew gathered around and gaped at it.

"Well, I never seen nothin' like it," admitted Sam after a few moments. The rest of the crew and Captain Mulligan all agreed that it was new to them as well. "What is it?"

"It's called a slingshot," Tom explained. "It's made of rubber and you put a smooth rock or a lead bullet in this leather patch, pull back, aim, and let fly.

"Well, I'll be a Barbary corsair," marveled Captain Mulligan. "And you can shoot that there slingshotty thing and hit what you're aiming at?'

"Now I can, but it took a lot of practice 'til I could hit exactly what I was shootin' at."

"All I can say is that without you and that slingshotty thing the *Decatur* would be lighting up the whole canal for a mile in both directions, and we would all be roastin' with her or floatin' in the water. I and the rest of the crew are mighty thankful to you Tom. Blessed was the thought I had when I asked you to travel with us. I can't tell you what this old boat means to me. If I'd lost it . . ."

"I only did what I thought I should do. I wanted to help, but I couldn't fight them any other way. So I just started shootin', hopin' I'd hit somethin'."

123

"You certainly hit something several times, judgin' by the sounds those raiders were makin'. I'll bet they have welts the size of watermelons and are wonderin' where they came from. It'll be a long time before they cross the river to raid the canal again, I can tell you."

"You know Captain," Sam interrupted, "it might be a good idea to get some of those slingshots and arm the crew with them. That old cutlass of yours and our two muskets aren't much against an armed party like we faced tonight. One man in the dark shooting from cover and not making any flash or noise would sure make a difference. Tom here proved that tonight."

"You may have something there, Sam. Tom, could you show us how to make them things and how to shoot them? I'd be obliged to you if you would."

"I guess so, but I'll need some rubber."

"I think we could probably get some in Washington City," Sam offered, "but it means, Tom, that you'll have to go with us to the end of the trip. You could cross the river at Harpers Ferry and be on your way to the army."

"I was going to tell you that, Tom," admitted Captain Mulligan, "but I didn't get around to it. I told you that I might have a way for you to get to the army at Fredericksburg. I know this sutler that sells all kinds of things to the soldiers. He runs his wagon out of Washington City and goes to the army on a regular basis to sell his wares. I'm sure I can get him to take you along."

Tom thought deep and hard. He wanted to reach his father as soon as he could but had to admit that he had no plan other than to get over the Potomac River somewhere. After that he didn't know what he would do. If Captain Mulligan had a friend who could take him right to the army that would solve his problem and he wouldn't have to walk all the way. Having made up his mind he said, "I'll go with you to Washington City."

"That's fine, Tom. Now, men, let's try to get a little sleep before the sun comes up."

"You want me to post a guard, Captain?" asked Sam.

"Tom," asked Captain Mulligan, "you got anymore of those lead bullets for that slingshotty thing of yours?"

"Yeah, about half a pouch full."

"No, Sam, we don't need a guard as long as we got Tom and his slingshotty thing to fight with us. Besides, I don't think those raiders want another taste of him, or it."

The remainder of the ninety-mile trip down the canal to Washington City took several days. Tom lived like a king. His work was light, Captain Mulligan often letting him just sit on the stern of the *Decatur* and fish for the crew's dinner. He ate and slept as well as he ever had at home. Sam let him guide the lead mule several times and when the boat stopped for the night, Captain Mulligan allowed him to leave the boat to look for suitable branch forks that could be used to make slingshots. At Harpers Ferry, the captain stopped the boat, having to report the attack of the raiders to the regional Union commander. Captain Mulligan took Tom with him. Tom had never seen so many soldiers in one place before. Not even General Stuart's long column of men could rival the thousands encamped around Harpers Ferry. They all were dressed in the same blue uniforms, and Tom began to wonder if he would recognize his father among the tens of thousands of soldiers that the army at Fredericksburg had. As they left, Tom looked back at the bridge that had spanned the river he needed to cross. A tinge of regret made him wish that he had not agreed to go on down the canal with Captain Mulligan, but he consoled himself with the knowledge that he would eventually cross the river and if Captain Mulligan was right, even have a way to travel to meet his father.

As the boat neared Washington City, Tom began to see huge fortifications with hundreds more blue-coated soldiers. Sam told him that the closer they got to Washington City the more soldiers and forts they would see. The boat's progress slowed. Twice it was stopped and boarded by officers who inspected the cargo and checked Captain Mulligan's papers and passes. Just outside of Georgetown, which was a town right next to Washington City, Captain Mulligan docked his boat near several very large buildings. He gave orders for the crew to unload the grain and place it on the dock where other men would load it in wagons to carry to one of the giant warehouses. "Tom," called Captain Mulligan, "you come with me."

If Tom had been by himself he would have been very scared. With so many buildings of all sizes, setting among a maze of streets, and what looked like hundreds of people, some with uniforms and others in work clothes, he soon got lost. But Captain Mulligan seemed to know exactly where he was going, so Tom followed along. Eventually they came to a warehouse near a long bridge that crossed the Potomac River. Tom's heart beat faster. Here at last was his way over the great barrier of water. Outside the warehouse stood dozens of wagons. Men were loading them with various sized boxes and barrels. Captain Mulligan stopped at the first wagon they came to and asked a man who had just put a barrel marked "Sugar" on the tailgate, "Is George Winslow about?"

"Seems like I saw George somewheres down that a way 'bout an hour ago," the burly man answered.

"Thank you. Come on Tom, I hope we can catch him."

Minutes later Captain Mulligan raised his arm, waved, and

126

shouted, "George! George Winslow, you old sea dog!"

A man with a red-gray beard, wearing a gold-braided cap very like the one worn by Captain Mulligan, looked down from his seat on a canvas-topped wagon and yelled back, "Mike Mulligan, you pirate you. Still stompin' around the deck of that flat bottomed excuse for a ship of yours?"

"The *Decatur* will still be a sea worthy craft long after the wheels fall off that land barge you've been sailin'."

Both men broke into hearty laughter as Mr. Winslow climbed down off the wagon and shook Captain Mulligan's hand until Tom thought he'd pull it off. "What's it been . . . weeks since we last set eyes on each other?" Mr. Winslow asked.

"More like a few months. How's the sutler business?"

"I've been doin' right well. Those army boys sure like my goods and enjoy the smiles I put on their faces. They like my prices, too. I keep them reasonable, being that I was once servin' our country like they are now."

"You're a good man, George. I'd like you to meet another good man." Turning toward Tom, Captain Mulligan said, "George, meet Tom. Don't know his last name. Don't want to, and you shouldn't either. Tom here is runnin' off to join his father in the army. I told him I might be able to get him a ride with you to Fredericksburg."

Finishing the introduction, Captain Mulligan added, "Tom, this here is my shipmate George Winslow. We fought together in the navy. He's captain of this here land schooner. Always did get seasick in a storm, didn't you George, so he got off the water and took to sailin' on dry ground."

"Looks like a right able lad," observed Mr. Winslow.

"More than able," explained Captain Mulligan. "The *Decatur* got jumped by raiders back above Lock 42. We were caught with our anchor in the water and half my crew on land. I had three of the scalawags after me when Tom here cut loose with his slingshotty thing and routed them. Sent them howling back across the river, he did."

"He used a what?"

"It's called a slingshot," interrupted Tom, pulling the weapon from his sack. Mr. Winslow looked at it rather quizzically, so Tom showed him how it worked.

A broad smile spread over Mr. Winslow's face as Captain Mulligan recounted the details of Tom's accurate fire. "There you have it, George. Now, will you give the boy a ride? He's mighty good with mules, so I suspect he is with horses as well. He could be of help to you on the way."

"That he could. I'm much better at haulin' in a jib than I am at takin' care of these beasts. I do all right by them, but I could sure use a hand. Gettin' a bit crickety in my bones. Sure I'll take him along."

Chapter 8

The Gray Ghost

E verything happened so fast it made Tom's head spin. One moment Captain Mulligan was asking Mr. Winslow if he would give Tom a ride to Fredericksburg, and the next minute Tom was sitting on the wagon next to Mr. Winslow, riding toward the big bridge over the Potomac River. Saying goodbye to Captain Mulligan took only a minute, leaving Tom little time to dwell on it. That was probably for the best, because had he the time, Tom would have found it very hard to do. Captain Mulligan, the *Decatur*, and its crew had grown to mean a great deal to him in the short time they had been together. Now as he rode across the bridge, Tom had time to think about how he really felt about them, and his eyes filled with tears. Wiping them away with the sleeve of his shirt, he said, "Thank you, Mr. Winslow, for agreein' to take me along with you. I . . ."

"Call me Captain George. This here four-wheeled scow is as much my ship as that old canal boat is to that pirate, Mulligan. My ship may not ride in the water, but she weathers all storms and sails over hill and dale like a good ship does through wind and wave."

Tom chuckled to himself and said, "Yes, sir, Captain George."

At the far end of the bridge, more soldiers stopped Captain George and looked in his wagon and at his papers and passes. They didn't seem to pay any attention to Tom at all. As he drove away, Captain

George speculated out loud, "Guess they don't consider a boy much of a threat. Can't say that I blame them. You look harmless enough. Good thing you didn't take that slingshotty thing out and plunk some of those soldier boys. That might've changed their minds."

"How long until we get to Fredericksburg?" asked Tom.

"As long as it takes. We're goin' to Annandale first. We'll join up with a couple of other sutlers there. It's safer if we travel together. Captain Mulligan has to deal with river raiders. We've got to deal with guerrillas."

"I read about them in school once. Big hairy apes. I didn't know we had them here."

"Not gorillas . . . guerrillas. . . partisans . . . They raid the army supply wagons and sutler wagons too. Steal everything they can get their hands on and carry it off. Mostly they want the horses, but if they have the inclination to, they'll take your wagon and leave you stranded with neither boots nor money. I've been mighty fortunate so far. Haven't had a run-in with any of them, but I know a couple of sutlers who lost all they had."

"Can't the army protect its wagons and you? I saw hundreds and hundreds of soldiers at Harpers Ferry and in Georgetown."

"Oh, the army tries, but the Rebels are too smart for them. They know this country like their own faces. They strike and fade away like the morning mist. Now don't you worry none about them. Captain George is prepared to repel all boarders."

The road to Annandale was crowded with wagons, soldiers marching this way and that, and regular citizens, all trying to get to and from Washington City. Not knowing exactly how far away Fredericksburg was, Tom began to think that if all the roads between it and Annandale were like the one they were on, it could take weeks. Captain George jawed away, telling one seafaring yarn after another. Some were funny. Others were scary. He had been in several sea battles, along with Captain Mulligan, who didn't like to talk about them. Captain George didn't mind sharing all the grizzly details of the fights with the Barbary pirates, some of which made Tom's hair stand on end, and made him wonder how Captain Mulligan and Captain George survived them.

The sun hung very low in the sky when Captain George pointed ahead to a cluster of buildings and said, "There be Annandale. Now all we got to do is find 'One Thumb' Dan Williams and 'Sadeye' Jim Beecher."

"Those are strange names?" marveled Tom.

"Well, they're not very strange fellows. Dan lost his left thumb in a shipboard accident and Jim just looks sad all the time. People just started to call them those names, and they got stuck with them. Best you call them by their real names after I introduce you. They'll be much obliged."

Finding Mr. Williams and Mr. Beecher among the scores of wagons parked around the little hamlet of Annandale proved a difficult task. Captain George left Tom with the wagon, telling him to guard it with his slingshotty thing, and went off in search of his two friends. Tom sat on the wagon seat, his slingshot and lead bullets at his feet, and stared into the growing gloom. His stomach growled at him, and he caught himself yawning several times. Still he was wide-awake when Captain George returned with good news. "Found them on the other side of town. They came in from Leesburg. We agreed to meet at the cross roads in the morning. Let's pull further off the road over there and set up camp for the night. Can you take care of the horses?"

By the time Tom had unhitched the horses, rubbed them down, and given them some feed, Captain George had started a cooking fire and made a delicious stew that Tom wolfed down along with some cold biscuits. With other wagons about and soldiers stationed along the road, Captain George felt they would be safe enough without taking turns standing guard. He gave Tom a bedroll and told him to sleep under the wagon. The day had been an exciting one. Tom lay awake for some time, thinking about how much closer he was to his father, and how far away he was from his mother and Ruth. For the first time since he had left home, he wondered if he had made the right decision and how his mother must have felt when she found out that he had run away. His stomach knotted. He pictured her sitting in the kitchen, crying. He rolled over and fought to blot the image from his mind. The fight tired him, and slowly he drifted off into a troubled sleep.

Dawn came with a flurry of activity. All around, cooking fires were burning and men were checking their wagons and hitching horses. Tom ate his eggs, bacon, and biscuits after he had hitched the horses to the wagon. Captain George chattered away about the coming day, and his hope of reaching the Telegraph Road near Accotink Creek before noon and the town of Occoquan by dark. The distance was only about fifteen miles, but with a fully loaded wagon and the roads being in poor repair, their progress would be slow.

When Captain George arrived at the road junction where they would take the road south, Mr. Beecher was waiting with bad news. Mr. Williams' wagon had broken down and it would be a few hours before he could fix it. "That's not good," said Captain George as Mr. Beecher walked away. "It means that we'll have to travel in a smaller group than I planned, just the three of us instead of about a dozen or so. It's safer to travel in larger groups, but I suppose we'll be all right. Well, let's not waste the time. Come on, we'll check to make sure everything is battened down in the wagon."

After about a half-dozen "make-sure-everything-is-battened-down" checks, Mr. Williams, who really was missing a thumb, and Mr. Beecher, who really looked sad, arrived, and the small train of three wagons turned south from Annandale toward the next hamlet of Springfield Station on the Orange and Alexandria Railroad. Outside Annandale the country immediately became very wooded. Tom, remembering Captain George's story about guerrillas, for a while watched every large tree that a man might hide behind. Captain George noticed and remarked, "If you keep starin' off into the woods like that you'll soon see things that ain't there. We bein' late might have been a good thing. The wagons that left before us will be a much more tempting target for the partisans than we will. No need to worry. I've taken this road a dozen times and never saw hide nor hair of a partisan." Somehow Captain George's words did nothing to calm Tom's growing fear. Having passed through one raid, he didn't want to go through another.

Springfield Station wasn't anything more than a small station and a couple of even smaller buildings. A group of about ten blue-clad infantry soldiers stood around as a guard, although Tom didn't see anything worth guarding other than the small station building itself. The three wagons passed through with a wave and a "Hello boys!" from Captain George to a corporal and two privates standing on the train platform. After crossing a creek, the land opened up a little, but Tom could see in the distance that the woods closed in again.

"We're comin' to the Old Fairfax Road in those woods up ahead," Captain George said, as if reading Tom's mind. "That's about halfway to the Telegraph Road. We're makin' good time. The smaller the number of wagons the faster you can go."

Tom didn't reply and as they entered the woods, he started to watch the trees again. Captain George nudged him and pointed

133

along the road. "Looks like a couple of troopers up ahead. They sometimes have pickets stationed at these cross roads to keep and eye out for partisans."

Captain George, driving the lead wagon, pulled up as he came to the two mounted men. They were dressed in blue and both had carbines that they rested on their thighs. "Good day," called out Captain George. Tom wondered if it was. He had seen mounted soldiers dressed in blue before, only they weren't friendly. A creepy-crawly feeling ran up and down his spine, and he slowly reached for his slingshot. He never got to it. Suddenly, the two soldiers pointed their carbines at Captain George and him and let out a whoop. The woods seemed to explode with men and quicker than Tom could count to ten, mounted men surrounded all three wagons. Captain George whispered to Tom, "Guess we weren't so safe after all."

A gray-uniformed man rode up to Captain George's wagon. He held no weapon in his hand and was armed only with a smile. He swept off a plumed hat very much like the one that Tom had seen General Stuart wear, and said in a calm voice, "My name is Captain John Mosby and you, your horses, wagons, and their contents are my prisoners. Please kindly step down."

Captain George whispered, "Mosby! The Gray Ghost!" followed by a very long, sad, sigh. He tied off the reins and climbed down from the seat. Tom reached down and picked up his sack and his slingshot and started to do the same. Captain Mosby stopped him with, "Wait a minute, boy. What's that you've got there?"

Tom sat back down on the wagon seat before answering, "What?"

"That object in your hand."

Tom held up his slingshot. "This?"

"Yes, what is it?"

"It's called a slingshot."

"I've heard of such a device. It's a weapon. Isn't it?"

"Yes, I guess so."

"Gentlemen," called out Captain Mosby to his men, "here is one of those things General Stuart told us about after his raid on Chambersburg. Remember? He said that a group of boys in one of the small towns attacked several of his men with slingshots and even knocked a few off their horses."

Three of the partisans came close to the wagon and stared at Tom and the slingshot in his hand. Slowly a strange look came over Captain Mosby's face, and Tom heard him mutter, "I wonder . . ." then ask, "What's your name, boy?"

"Thomas Jefferson Scott," Tom replied, his voice squeaking slightly as his throat tightened.

"Well I'll be . . . Men, unless I am mistaken this boy is the captain of those, now what did General Stuart call them . . . oh yes, the Mercersburg Invincibles." Looking Tom square in the eye, Captain Mosby asked, "Are you the boy who led the attack on General Stuart's troops?"

Tom gulped. He tried to talk, but nothing came out of his mouth. Finally, he nodded. Captain Mosby slapped his thigh, threw his head back, and roared with laughter. At first his men didn't understand, but between his bouts of laughter he managed to tell them that Tom was the very boy General Stuart had told them about. They all joined in. Once everyone had calmed down Captain Mosby continued, "From what General Stuart said, you and your Invincibles are brave young men, and that all of you conducted yourselves with courage and honor. It is a pleasure to meet you, Captain Scott," and Captain Mosby saluted.

Tom returned the salute automatically. His head whirled. He still was unsure exactly whether Captain Mosby, knowing that he was THE Captain Tom Scott of THE Mercersburg Invincibles was good or bad. If the last, what would that mean for him and for Captain George, Mr. Williams, and Mr. Beecher?

"What are you doing here in Virginia?" asked Captain Mosby.

Tom couldn't think of any reason why he shouldn't tell the truth. He couldn't get into any more trouble than he was already in. "I'm goin' to the army at Fredericksburg to see my father." He purposely left out the fact that he wanted to join the army as a drummer. No use in taking any chances, he thought.

"So your father is with the Yankee army at Fredericksburg? General Stuart told me that he met your pa and liked him too. What made him join the army?"

"General Stuart."

"General Stuart made your father join the Yankee army! Wait until I tell him he's been on recruiting duty for the Yankees. He'll get a laugh out of that. Were you planning to get there with this man?" Captain Mosby pointed to Captain George.

"Yes, he was kind enough to give me a ride, but I guess this is as far as I'm goin' to get."

"In these wagons, yes. I am afraid that I am going to have to take the horses and whatever my men want or can carry from the wagons and then burn them."

Captain George's face blanched white when he heard Captain Mosby. Mr. Williams and Mr. Beecher had been brought up to the front wagon and also heard what Captain Mosby said. They appeared just as shocked by the news. Tom knew he had to do something. "Captain Mosby, please don't burn their wagons. If you take the horses and whatever you want from the wagons won't that be enough? If you burn the wagons they won't have anything left."

"We are at war, Captain Scott."

136

"I know, but Captain George and Mr. Williams and Mr. Beecher aren't in the army. They just sell things to the soldiers."

"At ridiculous prices, no doubt."

"Our prices are very fair," yelled Captain George, before he realized what he was saying.

"Be that as it may," said Captain Mosby, "if you are not in the army, why did the boy call you Captain George?"

"He used to be in the navy," Tom explained. "This wagon is his ship now, his home, too. He sails it over hill and dale just like he . . ."

"I understand." After a long pause, Captain Mosby added, "I will spare their wagons on one condition. You allow me to take you to your father."

Tom nearly fell off the wagon seat. He had already been taken prisoner once by the infernal Confederate Rebels, and now here he was about to be taken prisoner again by another infernal Confederate Rebel. Captain Mosby went on, "I'd like you to show my men how that slingshot of your works. And, I'd like to hear your side of the great fight between the Mercersburg Invincibles and General Stuart's men. I want to make sure General Stuart's story matches with yours. Right men." All those who heard chuckled.

"Captain Mosby," interrupted Captain George, "this boy was placed in my care. I know I don't have any way of influencing your decision, but I cannot permit you to take him with you."

"Did the boy's mother place him in your care?"

"No," shouted Tom, "I ran away from home. I came down the canal to Georgetown, and the canal boat captain asked Captain George to take me to my father."

"I see. Well, my offer still stands. Tom, I give you my word here in front of your friends and my men that I will deliver you safely to your father at Fredericksburg and that I will not burn these wagons. In fact, I will leave their contents undisturbed and only take the horses."

"But Captain Mosby . . ." pleaded Captain George.

If Tom could have willed himself back home at that very instant he would have, and he also gladly would have taken any punishment his mother wanted to give him. But he couldn't go back. In his wildest dreams, he never thought when he ran away that he would go through all that he had. That one decision, made, he knew now, without really thinking about the consequences, had put him here, in this very spot, with so much at stake. Then a thought flashed into his head. Captain Mosby had said that General Stuart had told him the Mercersburg Invincibles had behaved bravely, with courage and honor. That was what he must do now. If he could save Captain George's, Mr. Williams's, and Mr. Beecher's wagons by going with Captain Mosby, then go he must. "I'll go with you."

"But Tom, you can't go with these men," argued Captain George.

"If I don't, you'll lose your wagons and Mr. Williams and Mr. Beecher will lose theirs, too. I can't let that happen. I'll be safe. Captain Mosby promised . . ."

"But can you trust him? He's the enemy."

"General Stuart was the enemy too, and he kept his word."

That ended the discussion. Captain Mosby ordered his men to unhitch the horses. Tom climbed down from the wagon and up onto one of the horses. None of the Rebels entered any of the wagons. Tom, his sack and slingshot in his hands, waved goodbye to Captain George, Mr. Williams, and Mr. Beecher. Captain George shouted, "Thank you, Tom, for saving our wagons. You're as brave a sailor as I ever met."

At that moment Tom didn't feel very brave. Truth was that his stomach had turned over several dozen times, and he was sweating freely even though there was an April chill in the air. Captain Mosby doffed his plumed hat to the three sutlers and called, "It's not such a long walk back to the station. You can telegraph for more horses from there, and don't worry, I and my men will be long gone from here by the time they arrive. But perhaps we may meet again."

As they had come, so they went. Captain Mosby and his men melted into the trees, this time with Tom in tow. In a few minutes, he could not even see the road. No wonder the partisans had such success. If they knew these woods like their own faces, as Captain George had said, they could go anywhere, strike at any target, and escape practically unseen. The Rebels talked little until they came to what looked like a narrow trail. From what Tom could judge from where the sun stood in the sky, Captain Mosby led his small band south. *At least I'm going in the right direction,* Tom thought.

Entering a small clearing, Tom saw that the group of wagons that had gone ahead of them from Annandale had not escaped Captain Mosby either. Several dozen horses, still partly in harness, stood about loaded with all kinds of goods from cloth, to boots, to boxes of canned fruit, and much more. Captain Mosby saw Tom staring and rode over to him. "We caught them just short of the Telegraph Road. We didn't burn the wagons because it would have alerted any soldiers on the road that we were in the area. Your friends' wagons would have been far enough away that no one would have noticed right away, giving us plenty of time to escape. So, you see, you really did save them."

Tom felt better and asked, "Where are you taking me?"

"Where I promised to take you . . . to your father. However, I cannot tell you exactly when you'll arrive. I do not travel on the normal byways, as you have seen for yourself. My men and I like to take paths and side roads that are little used, or unfamiliar to the Yankees. I will get you there. Just not as fast as Captain George would have. I hope that doesn't matter."

"As long as I get there."

For the rest of the day Captain Mosby and his men wound their way along forest tracks, farm lanes, and narrow seldom used roads. Scouts always went ahead to check for the enemy, and some men always hung back to make sure the column would not be surprised from the rear. As they rode, Captain Mosby trotted up and down his column of men, joking, laughing, and giving orders when necessary. He finally joined Tom and rode with him for a time. At first, Tom kept silent, but finally his curiosity got the better of him and he asked, "Why do they call you the Gray Ghost? Did you give yourself that name?"

"I can honestly say," replied Captain Mosby, "that the name originates with my blue-coated friends. I suppose it refers to my appearing and disappearing among them. I guess you could say I haunt them."

"Do you like it?"

"If it means that I have somewhat succeeded in unnerving them and causing them to look over their shoulders to see if I am there, yes. Otherwise, it means little. A soldier such as I is only as good as his last raid, and each raid may be his last. It is a dangerous game, Tom; one not to be played lightly."

"Why do you do it then?"

"I am not much for drilling and lying about camp with nothing to do. I tried that once, and it didn't suit. This is what I do best, and it helps my people. But I must see to finding a camp for the night. Remember we all want to hear your story about fighting General Stuart's troopers. Be ready."

Around a small fire, eating from some of the canned food they had taken from the sutlers, Captain Mosby and his men sat waiting for Tom to finish chewing the last of his canned oysters. Tom took his time, all the while thinking back to that October day when he and the Invincibles got caught up in the turmoil of General Stuart's ride through Mercersburg. He hoped that he could not only tell the story well but also that it would agreed with what General Stuart had told Captain Mosby. Of course, Tom did not know what had been told, so all he could do was tell what he remembered and hope that it was the same or close to the same. He swallowed the last of the oysters and dropped the can into the fire.

"Now Tom," called out Captain Mosby, "just exactly what happened between your men and General Stuart's?"

Tom told his tale. In the beginning he stuttered and paused. But before too long, he saw that his audience was listening to his every word, and he warmed to the telling. The men doubled over with laughter several times, especially when Tom told of Private Griggs being knocked off his horse. When he had finished his audience gave him a round of quiet applause so as "not to give our position away," as Captain Mosby explained. Everyone decided that Tom's story was much better than General Stuart's who had left out all the good parts. Tom lay down to sleep that night, his stomach full and his hopes high. He had come to trust Captain Mosby and his men, as he had trusted General Stuart.

Tom awoke to find many of Captain Mosby's men and most of the captured horses gone. During breakfast, several new men came into camp from different directions until there were almost as many men as there had been the night before. Captain Mosby explained that he had learned of another sutler train and that he intended to attack it. Tom would be taken to another hidden camp while the raid took place. Captain Mosby would meet him there.

The ride only added to Tom's confusion about where exactly he was. His guide said almost nothing and would not or could not answer any of Tom's questions. Although the general direction of their travel was south, they wound this way and that through

141

the same kind of back trails and narrow roads as they had the day before, leaving Tom with no idea of how he got where they finally ended up – at a small farm. Hidden in the barn eating some food brought by a kind lady, Tom had plenty of time to think. His mind raced over several subjects before settling on his father and what he would say to him when they met. Strangely, that thought had never entered into Tom's head before that moment. What **would** he say to his father when he showed up out of nowhere? Almost instantly Tom realized that his father might not see things the same way Tom did. If he didn't, then what? Tom began to plan exactly what he would say when he saw his father. He was still deep in thought when a commotion outside the barn interrupted him.

"Yankees," Tom's guide whispered down from the hayloft. "Quick, hide over there behind those sacks. I've hidden our horses in the woods so they shouldn't find them. If we're quiet they won't find us neither."

Tom, having grown quite good at hiding since leaving home, slipped behind the sacks and even had time to pull a couple of them over him before the barn door flew open.

"We know you've been harborin' men from Mosby's band, Mrs. Chappel," Tom heard one of the soldiers say. "Things'll go easier on you if you just tell us where Mosby is."

"How could I know that," Mrs. Chappel argued. "Captain Mosby doesn't tell me or anyone else his plans, as any fool should know."

"If you refuse to cooperate, my men will have to search the house and this here barn. No tellin' what kind of damage they may do tearin' things apart lookin' for Rebels."

"Got nothin' to hide. You can see I ain't got a horse on the place. I ain't even got a huntin' rifle to shoot squirrels. I'm nearly starved from you Yankees stealin' every hog and chicken I got. You can't do much more to me than you've done already."

The Union soldier growled some words Tom could not understand and then said, "All right men, mount up. Maybe we'll find somethin' at the next place. Mosby can't hide from us forever."

"You better hope he can," called Mrs. Chappel as the soldiers mounted their horses. "You may not enjoy catchin' up with him as much as you think."

The sound of hoofbeats gradually grew fainter and fainter. Tom peeked out from under the sacks and saw Mrs. Chappel standing in the open door of the barn, looking off down the lane. She didn't turn or move as she said, "Better stay where you are for a spell. I've known them to go off down the road and then turn around and come right back, hopin' to surprise me or my guests. I'll come back and tell you when it's safe to move. Then you better be goin'. I'll tell Captain Mosby that you've moved on. I reckon he'll know where to find you."

About a half hour later Mrs. Chappel opened the barn door a crack and said quietly, "Better be off now."

Once again on their horses, Tom and his guide trotted away from the farm along another of the woodland paths used by Captain Mosby and his men. "My name is Daniel Jeffords," Tom's guide called back to him over his shoulder. "How come you didn't give us away back there? Those Yanks would have taken you to your pa and may have rewarded you for turnin' me in."

The question caught Tom off guard. *Why hadn't he alerted the soldiers?* Tom had to think for a few moments before answering, "Captain Mosby gave me his word to take me to my pa. If those men found out I had run away from home they might have just sent me back and . . . I like all of you, even if you are Rebels."

Daniel chuckled but said nothing more. They rode on in silence until after dark. Only Daniel's knowledge of the trails allowed them to continue. About an hour after the sun had set they rode out into a clearing. The light from a window glowed a few hundred yards away. "You stay here with the horses," Daniel ordered. "I'll go and see if our farmer friend has any unwanted company."

Minutes dragged by as Tom waited in the darkness, alone except for the horses. They were as quiet as he, perhaps somehow knowing the danger their human riders were in. Just when Tom was about to dismount and go looking for Daniel a shadowy form appeared out of nowhere. "It's all right, Tom. It's me, Daniel. Captain Mosby is over there in that barn." Tom strained to see the structure through the dim starlight. "He spotted the Yankees comin' from Mrs. Chappel's farm and seein' that we wasn't with them, he figured I would bring you here as planned."

"Well, Tom," exclaimed Captain Mosby as Tom entered the barn, "you are one for getting into all kinds of scrapes! Seems like you go from one adventure to another."

"I guess so," admitted Tom, "but I don't mean to. They sort of just happen to me."

"Thank you for not turning in Private Jeffords. He's a fine young soldier and I'd hate to lose him. Now as to what we must do with you."

"Me?"

"Yes, Tom, but have no fear. I am just concerned that your talent for getting into difficulty might prevent me from delivering you to your father as I promised. Therefore, we will leave tomorrow morning and go directly, as directly as we can, to Fredericksburg. Besides, this last little sting we inflicted on the Yanks has made things a trifle uncomfortable around here. It's best if we leave this area for a time."

"So, tomorrow you're takin' me to the army at Fredericksburg?"

"Yes and no."

CHAPTER 9

Reunion

I f Tom had expected to see his father the very next day, he would have been greatly disappointed. However, Captain Mosby's "yes and no," answer had given warning that getting to Fredericksburg would not be a simple task. Fortunately, Tom's journey thus far had prepared him for the unexpected. Indeed, it had been one unexpected event after another since he had left home. Therefore, the three-day roundabout tour of the northeastern part of Virginia's back roads and trails came as no surprise. It seemed that one man or another of Captain Mosby's little band knew every human and animal trail through every wood and forest, every ford of every stream, and every hiding place for every mile between Annandale and Fredericksburg. Tom suspected that they would have known all of them no matter what direction they might have traveled.

Now that he knew for certain that he was soon to see his father, Tom enjoyed the trip. His only problem came from his inability to come up with what he would tell his father when he saw him. Tom decided that any kind of a lie would not be a good idea. He knew the truth was the best way to go. But how to tell the truth, that was the big question. Just blurting it out might not be the best thing to do. What kept Tom up nights and occupied during the days was trying to find the right way to tell the truth - a soft, safe way, a way that would not make his father send him packing back home the minute he saw him. By the third day of the ride, Tom had managed to devise no plan whatsoever to tell his father why he had come, other than the cold hard truth – he had run away from home to be with him, and wanted to join the army as a drummer boy. The thought didn't make Tom feel very good.

As Captain Mosby's small band neared Fredericksburg, Tom noticed that the pace they had been traveling slowed to almost a crawl. Captain Mosby explained that the closer one came to the Yankee army, the more the roads were guarded, making it very difficult to get near it without being seen. In the woods near the Potomac Creek – Tom thought it very strange that the first great barrier between him and his father had been the Potomac River, and now this last one was a creek by the same name – Captain Mosby called a halt late in the afternoon of the third day. He sent out scouts that came back and reported finding a picket post where the creek crossed the road from Stafford Court House to Falmouth. "Just as I thought," Captain Mosby muttered. Turning to Tom he added, "That's where we'll deliver you, Tom. You can understand, I am sure, why we don't want to get too close to so large a force of the enemy."

Tom smiled and said, "I understand."

"Now you need to know that what I'm planning to do won't be easy and you'll have to be very brave for us to do it at all."

"I don't understand."

"Tonight two of my men, dressed as Yankees, will take you out on the road and ride toward the picket post. They will pretend to be members of one of the Yankee cavalry regiments camped near here. They will call out to the picket and explain that they have you and that you want to see your father. You will need to confirm their story. Otherwise . . ."

"What do you mean?"

"Good pickets are on the alert for anything strange. That's why you will be taken late at night, so the picket can't see too well. You will have to help convince the picket that my men are really Yankee cavalry, delivering you to your father."

"I'll say whatever you want me to say."

"Good boy. Now, we have a few hours. Suppose you show us how that slingshot of yours works."

Being near the creek permitted Tom to gather a number of smooth pebbles to use while he demonstrated how to load, aim, and fire a slingshot. If he had not, his supply of lead bullets would have quickly been exhausted, as every one of the men wanted to try his hand with the unusual weapon. Some were better than others. Some were plain awful, causing considerable amusement, but they kept as quiet as possible so as not to reveal the tiny band's presence to the enemy. Like General Stuart, Captain Mosby attempted a few shots, missing his target each time, though coming close. A dinner of canned fruit followed, Captain Mosby not allowing any fire to be lit.

When the time came to leave, Tom saw that one of the men going with him was Daniel. The other was Corporal Zack Foster. Captain Mosby clasped Tom's hand and said, "I will tell General Stuart about our little adventure. I am sure he will approve of my helping you. He will, that is, if all goes well. Once you reach your father you may tell him and anyone else how you arrived here. I only wish I could see the Yanks faces when you reveal that my men and I were involved."

The road lay shrouded in darkness. Captain Mosby had accompanied Tom and his two men that far, giving final instructions to all before disappearing back into the trees along the road where he promised to wait for his men's return. Before he left he saluted Tom whispering, "I'm glad my men and I did not have to face your

Invincibles and those slingshots. I don't think we would have fared any better than General Stuart's men did. Goodbye and good luck."

Tom, Daniel, and Zack rode along the narrow ribbon of road, making no attempt to conceal their presence. Captain Mosby had told them to ride as if they were out in broad daylight. The picket would hear them coming and would be on his guard. The noise would help convince him that everything was normal. Partisans would advance quietly. Having come out of the woods only a mile from where the picket stood, it did not take long before a voice came out of the darkness, "Halt! Advance and give the countersign."

Zack replied, "Don't know no countersign. We're from the Eight New York Cavalry. Been out on patrol, looking for that Gray Ghost feller for four days. Didn't find so much as a hoofprint. But we got a boy here whose tryin' to find his pa. Says he's here in the army. What regiment did you say your pa was in, boy?"

Tom's mind went blank for a second or two before he managed to say, "The Fifty-sixth Pennsylvania. My pa's name is Jonathan Scott. My uncle is in the same regiment. His name is Jeremiah Reynolds."

Only a deathly quiet came from the direction of the creek. Zack called out again, 'We ain't got all night. My sergeant'll give us the devil if we don't get back before daylight. Will you take the boy to his pa or not?'

"Corporal of the Guard," Tom heard the picket yell out, followed by, "Stand where you are. If you move, I'll fire."

A splashing sound and muffled voices were all that Tom could hear. Daniel and Zack sat quietly, not moving a muscle. One of their horses whinnied. It sounded like a thunderclap in the quiet of the night. More muffled talking filtered to them through the blackness. Finally, a voice came to them strong and clear. "Send the boy forward on foot. We hear anything but one set of legs walking and we fire."

Tom slid off his mount. Knees shaking and with sweat pouring down his face, neck, and back, he walked forward as naturally as possible. Glancing back over his shoulder Tom couldn't find Daniel or Zack in the shadow of the great tree they had stopped under. Looking ahead, he couldn't see anything but the center of the narrow road. The sound of the creek grew stronger. Without warning a man holding a musket leveled right at Tom stepped from behind a tree at the right of the road. Another came from the left.

"Well, I'll be," the musket soldier mumbled. "It IS a boy."

"You men on the horses," called out the Corporal of the Guard. "You just turn around and ride off. If you try to come any closer, we'll fire."

Tom heard Zack yell back, "Ain't got no reason to come closer. We delivered our package." The sounds of horses moving away along the road told Tom that his friends had left him. Once more he was in the company of strangers.

"You say your pa is in the Fifty-sixth Pennsylvania?" the corporal asked.

"Yes, and my uncle, too."

"I'll take you across the stream, but you'll have to wait there under guard until my officer comes on his rounds."

"Sure."

Being patience had never been something that Tom did well, but he was getting better at it. He certainly had been getting plenty of practice. Now that he was so close to his father, he wanted to rush on. Knowing he couldn't, he sat in the dark waiting. Other than the mute corporal, only the sounds of the creek and the woods kept him company. Tom thought about trying to start a conversation, but decided against it. What would he say? Best to keep quiet, he reasoned.

The sound of footsteps caused Tom to jump up, and brought an immediate response from the corporal, "You just sit back down, boy. That'll be my officer. He'll decide what to do with you."

"What's the trouble, corporal?"

The Corporal of the Guard recounted everything that had happened from the time the picket had called "Halt!" Tom could just make out the officer glancing at him from time to time as if trying to figure out what to make of him. Tom caught only snatches of the conversation, nothing making any sense to him. At last the officer came over to Tom and leaning down said, "Come with me, boy. I hope you've been telling the truth or you and I are both going to be in a great deal of trouble. No one is supposed to pass through the picket line without specific orders. I don't suppose you even have a pass."

"What's a pass?"

"Thought not. Listen. Don't talk unless you are asked a question and then tell the truth. If you don't know, say so."

Tom was amazed at all the men guarding the road behind the picket post. He received stares and a few, "We're sure draftin' them young, ain't we," from some of the soldiers sitting in front of roaring campfires. The officer guided him to a tent with two soldiers standing guard in front of it. "Wait here," the officer said. From inside the tent, Tom heard, "What is it, Lieutenant?"

"Sir, there's a boy outside. He came through our picket on the Stafford road. Some men of the Eighth New York Cavalry brought him in. He says he is looking for his father in the Fifty-sixth Pennsylvania. I brought him . . ."

"Lieutenant, your orders are to permit no one to pass in or out through your pickets. What part of those orders do you fail to understand?"

"Major, I thought . . ."

"Our government doesn't pay you to think, Lieutenant. It pays you to follow orders, which you obviously have difficulty in doing. However, since he's here, I'll take a look at him. Bring the boy in."

"Yes, Sir."

The lieutenant held open the tent flap for Tom to enter. A man sat behind a table on which lay several piles of papers. The man rose and walked around the table, all the while staring at Tom. "You told the lieutenant that your father is in the Fifty-sixth Pennsylvania? Is that true?"

"Yes . . . and my uncle too."

"Where did you come from?"

"I live in Mercersburg, that's in Pennsylvania, with my ma and little sister. Her name is Ruth. I ran away to be with my pa and join the army as a drummer boy."

The major chuckled. "So you want to be a drummer boy, do you? I don't think your pa would approve of that. How did you meet up with the Eighth New York?"

"I didn't."

"Lieutenant, you stated that the boy was brought to the picket post by the Eighth New York Cavalry. He says he never met up with them. What's going on here?"

Tom broke in. "He told me that after I got to be with my pa I could tell you . . . but I guess I can tell you now. Captain Mosby brought me here."

"Mosby! The Gray Ghost brought you here! You mean he was right out there in front of my pickets?"

"No, he was back up the road. He sent two of his men to bring me to the picket."

"Lieutenant, the less I know of this matter the better. Take the boy up to brigade headquarters and for goodness sake don't let him mention Mosby to anyone. I don't relish another rebuke from the colonel or the general. The less said the better. Understand?"

"I believe I do, Sir."

"And boy, you won't mention Mosby to anyone, including your father, will you?"

"No, Sir."

Even though it was the middle of the night, the general's tent glowed bright from the lamps inside it. Several other tents that surrounded it also were lit up. Guards stood all around the area, and the lieutenant had to show some papers to another officer to be permitted to enter the area. Again, the lieutenant ordered Tom to wait outside the tent. When he was waved inside, he was pushed in front of a very large table behind which sat a very thin, bearded man chewing on a biscuit. The lieutenant did all the talking, never mentioning that the troopers from the Eighth New York Cavalry had actually been men of Mosby's command. After the lieutenant had finished the general said, "The Fifty-sixth is in Hofmann's brigade. They're camped about a mile and a half down the road outside of Falmouth."

"Am I to see the boy there, Sir?"

"Of course, Lieutenant. We can't have him stumbling around in the dark. Some fool will shoot him for a partisan."

"Yes, Sir."

Outside, the lieutenant said, "You . . .say, what's your name?"

"Thomas Jefferson Scott."

"Well, Thomas Jefferson Scott, you certainly are a considerable amount of trouble. By the time I take you to the Fifty-sixth and I get back to my regiment it'll be dawn, and I'll have gone the entire night without a wink of sleep."

"I'm sorry."

"It's all right, and thanks for not mentioning about . . . you know.

The major and I would really be in for it then."

"I promise I won't tell anyone."

For the entire mile and a half, the lieutenant chattered away on one subject after another. By the time they reached the camp of Colonel Hofmann's brigade, Tom knew the lieutenant's entire life story, or so it seemed. Colonel Hofmann had little to say other than for the lieutenant to take Tom to Colonel Hofmann, commander of the Fifty-sixth. Once there, the lieutenant wasted no time in bidding Tom farewell and disappearing into the night.

Colonel Hofmann, who looked to Tom to be about the same age as his father, questioned him thoroughly. He wanted to know just about everything from the time Tom left home until the moment he stepped into the Colonel's tent. Tom managed to avoid any mention of Captain Mosby, but otherwise spoke truthfully. The colonel didn't say anything when Tom told him that he wanted to join the army as a drummer boy, although he did stare at Tom and shake his head slightly. When he had finished, the colonel called in one of the guards and gave him an order to bring Private Scott of Company D to him. Not another word was spoken by Tom or Colonel Hofmann while they waited.

The man that stepped into the colonel's headquarters tent was not Private Jonathan Scott. In fact, Tom would have sworn an oath that he had never seen the man before in is life. After saluting Colonel Hofmann the stranger looked at Tom and said, "Why Tom, don't you know me? It's your Uncle Jeremiah." Only after the man spoke his name did Tom recognize him. He had changed so much since Tom had seen him two years before.

"Uncle Jeremiah? I didn't know you."

"Well, army life will do that to you. I barely know myself when I see my reflection in a pool of water. What are you doing here?"

Not seeing his father behind Jeremiah caused Tom a moment of panic, and he blurted out, "Where's my pa? Did somethin' happen to him? Take me to my pa!"

"Your pa's fine. He's on guard duty. He'll be back in a couple of hours." Jeremiah again addressed Colonel Hofmann. "With your permission, Colonel, I'll take the boy to our tent. He can wait for his father there."

"Very well, Private, but this problem must be resolved quickly. I can't permit family members to visit my men anytime they feel like it, especially now."

"I understand, sir. I am sure that Private Scott will handle the problem to your satisfaction."

"And, Thomas, isn't it?" Colonel Hofmann called as Tom left the tent. "This regiment has all the drummers it needs."

Waiting at the fire next to the small shelter that Jeremiah and Jonathan called home, Tom could barely sit still for worrying about seeing his father, unable to decide, now that he was faced with it, whether he wanted to or not. Half of his conscience anchored him in front of the flickering flames while the other half pulled at him to run back to Mosby's camp and ask to be taken back to where he had been captured. He could get home from there, he was sure. Uncle Jeremiah asked several questions to which Tom gave no answers that made any sense, and Jeremiah stopped talking.

"Thomas!" came a voice from the darkness beyond the fire. "Thomas! What are you doing here? Where is your mother? Where is Ruth? How did . . .? Why on earth . . .?" Jonathan Scott stooped over Tom, grabbed him by the arms, and lifted him to his feet. If it had not been for the voice, Tom would not have known him. Jonathan Scott had changed. Thinner, bearded, somewhat grimy, and clothed in a coat that hung on bony shoulders, he no longer looked like the man Tom knew.

"Pa! Pa?" Tom managed to say, his thoughts all a jumble.

"Where are your mother and Ruth? Why did you come down here?"

"We didn't. I mean she didn't. They didn't. I did. Ma and Ruth are back home."

"She let you come here alone! Why? For what reason? Is something wrong with Ruth?"

"They're all right. I guess. They were when I left."

"Didn't your mother send you?"

"No, I . . . I ran away. I wanted . . . to be with you. I want . . . to join the army as a drummer, but Colonel Hofmann said that . . ."

"You . . . you ran away? You left your mother and Ruth to . . . to . . ."

"Ma has Ruth. You got nobody. I want to be with you."

"Thomas, how could you leave your mother like this? She is probably sick with worry. She needs you to help run the farm, to plant the crops, to . . . Thomas, what have you done."

"But you need me too. Don't you? I missed you. I want to be with you. I can be a drummer. Talk to Colonel Hofmann. Make him . . ."

"Thomas! Believe me when I say that I want to be with you and your mother and Ruth more that I can . . . but I can't. And you can't be here with me. You have no idea what being a drummer boy means or the dangers that you would have to face. I couldn't do my duty, worrying about what might happen to you. Neither could Jeremiah."

"You . . . you don't want me to stay?"

"It's not about what I want or about what you want. It is about what must be done. I must stay here with the army. You must go home to your mother and Ruth. They need you more than I. I can't protect you here, but if I know all of you are home safe, it will help me do what I must do."

Tom pulled out of his father's grip and stepped back. His anger welled up inside him. He flung himself forward and beat his fists against his father's chest. Tears flooded down his cheeks as he sobbed and poured out his fury. His father reached out and drew Tom close. The two slumped down by the fire. "I know this is hard for you to understand," Jonathan whispered into his son's ear, "but your mother needs you right now. Who can she depend on if both of us are gone? I can't go home. You can. You must take care of her and Ruth for me until I get back. Then I can take care of all of you again like I did before this terrible war came into our lives."

Tom looked up into his father's face, a face he hardly recognized. What he saw there was love, fear, and a longing that told Tom everything he needed to know. "I'll go back, but can I stay with you tomorrow. I'm very tired."

When Tom awoke the sun hung in the middle of the sky and the camp was bustling with activity. For several moments, he could not find his father and then noticing him at a tent a few yards away ran to him.

"I'm happy you're awake," Jonathan said. "I was about to come and get you up. I've arranged for you to ride the supply train back to Washington City. It will leave in about a half an hour."

"You're sendin' me home already. I thought maybe that I could stay awhile and . . ."

"No, Thomas. You can't stay. Rumors say that the army will move out on campaign soon. I want you safely away from here before that."

"Pa, I . . ."

"We've already talked about this. Remember? You must go home."

"I remember."

"I asked Colonel Hofmann if he would give you a pass so that

156

you could ride the train to Washington City. Civilians usually are not permitted to ride on military trains. He worked things out somehow. I think he is every bit as anxious to get you out of here as I am. Now, I will give you enough money to get you home. You'll have to take a canal boat from Washington City to Williamsport. From there you can travel by coach to Hagerstown and from there by railroad to Greencastle. Another coach will then get you back to Mercersburg. Do you think you can do this by yourself?"

"Pa, I got all the way here by myself without any money."

Jonathan Scott chuckled before admitting, "So you did. When I get home you must tell me how you did it, but this time, please . . ."

"I'll do everythin' just like you said, Pa. Honest."

"And don't worry about me. Remember, I am not here alone. I have Uncle Jeremiah for company. We'll take care of each other. And remember, you must take care of your mother and Ruth."

"I will."

His pass pinned to his shirt, Tom stood next to the train, feeling much like a package about to be shipped off to some relative. The supplies the train had brought, now stacked in huge piles, surrounded him on three sides. The empty train cars were being loaded with sick soldiers going to hospitals in Baltimore and Washington City and troops, headed for where Tom had no idea. His father pressed some money into Tom's hand cautioning, "Don't let anyone see this. There should be enough for your tickets and a few meals."

"Pa, I'm sorry. I . . ."

"Save your apologies for your mother, Thomas. She is the one who should receive them. I'm just thankful you got here safely. I shudder when I think of what might have happened to you if you had run into that Gray Ghost Mosby fellow or one of his kind. Your mother and I may never have seen you again."

157

Tom fought to hold back his laughter, thankfully managing to do so, though he had to turn around slowly in a complete circle and pretend to be looking at all the supplies. He so very badly wanted to defend Captain Mosby, but remembering his promise he said only, "Your army really eats a lot."

"Yes, it does," his father agreed.

Once on the train, Tom leaned out the window and took his father's hand. "I'll get home, Pa. Don't worry."

"Give my love to your mother and Ruth. Tell them, I'm fine and will write as soon as I can and . . ."

The train's shrill whistle drowned out the rest of his father's words, and with a heavy jerk the train pulled away. Tom kept his eyes on his father until he was just a speck standing beside a narrow ribbon of track. The tears that filled Tom's eyes were not over his long journey home, but for what he had wanted so badly and now understood he could not have. Yes, his father needed him, but his mother needed him more. How could he not have known that, he wondered? Something deep within told him that going home would be much more difficult than running away had been.

At Washington City Tom hoped to find Captain Mulligan. If he could, he would be able to save some money because he was sure that the captain would let him ride his boat for free. Tom searched and searched and asked and asked, but no one knew where Captain Mulligan could be found. After wasting a whole morning, Tom bought a ticket on a passenger boat and began the journey west. This one wasn't nearly as exciting as his last, although several of Tom's fellow travelers talked about a terrible raid on one of the canal boats they had heard about. They told about some boy, armed only with a stick, who single handedly drove back two dozen raiders, capturing five of them. When one of passengers said that the name of the boat was the *Decatur,* Tom almost choked on the biscuit he was eating. Whether Captain Mulligan was spreading around a wild story or what he had told had grown with each repetition by those who heard it, Tom could not tell, but he sat and listened very intently to hear what a hero he was and that President Lincoln himself was hoping to find out the identity of the boy so he could give him a reward. That night Tom went to sleep with a big smile on his face.

On the coach ride from Williamsport to Hagerstown, Tom shared a seat with a wounded officer who was traveling home. As bad as Tom wanted to ask him questions about what had happened to him, something told him not to. For the entire trip the soldier sat and stared out the coach window, a far away look in his eyes.

The train from Hagertsown to Greencastle chugged along slowly, providing Tom with the opportunity to think about what he was going to say to his mother when he saw her. While riding with Captain Mosby through the back roads of Virginia, he had not enjoyed the experience of trying to find something to tell his father, and this time was no different – only maybe it was worse. He had not run away from his father but to him. He **had** run away from his mother. Were there any words that could explain that, he wondered? If there were, he didn't know them.

The last few miles to Mercersburg, jostling along in the coach, were the worst. His heart pounded on the inside of his chest, doing everything it could to escape, as if it didn't want any part of what he must face. His head ached from thinking but was as empty of answers to his problem as it was when he first began to think about seeing his mother again. Other thoughts, all unpleasant ones, battled in his mind. Would she talk to him? Would she even look at him? Would she send him away? And then, suddenly, the coach abruptly stopped. Tom peered out the window to see Colonel Murphy's hotel. He was back in Mercersburg, where everything had started. He froze. The coach driver had to practically lift him from his seat because none of Tom's muscles seemed to be working properly.

Standing in the street, Tom shut his eyes. The sounds of the town filtered into his brain. "Good afternoon, Mrs. . . ." "How's that sick horse of yours, Mr. . . ." "Luckily we caught the fire before it got to the hay in the barn." None of the voices sounded familiar until, "Tom? Tom! You're back!" Opening his eyes, Tom saw Jake standing in the middle of Franklin Street with the funniest look on his face Tom had ever seen. "Jake! Jake!" Tom cried. The two boys ran toward each other, nearly colliding. For several seconds they simply stood facing each other, staring as if each had seen a ghost. "Your pa didn't let you stay?" Jake asked when he again found his vocal chords.

"No," answered Tom dejectedly.

"I didn't think he would. Was he mad?"

"No."

"You seen your ma yet?"

"No. Just got off the coach."

"What're you goin' to say to her?"

"I've been tryin' to think of what to say but . . . What did you say to your ma?"

"Just that I was sorry for runnin' away and that I'd never do it again and that I lov . . . Well, you know."

"Yeah, I know, but I ain't sure that's goin' to be enough for what I did."

CHAPTER 10

Homecoming

J ake walked with Tom beside the creek to the old tree where the
Invincibles had met to drill and practice with their slingshots.
Neither boy spoke. Jake didn't know what to say, and Tom
was too absorbed with the thought of seeing his mother to
make small talk. At the tree, they parted, although Jake stayed to
watch his friend cross the field. Tom never looked back. Had he, he
would have seen Jake waving. His lieutenant knew what his captain
was about to face, having done the same, and that he would need
every ounce of courage he possessed to do it. Remembering his own
reunion with his mother, Jake's eyes filled with tears as he turned for
home.

Tom went back the way he had gone, through the barn. He paused
at his secret hiding place, crouching down to drop in his slingshot,
ammunition pouch, and a few other things. Then he stood up and
took several deep breaths. It wasn't that the walk had exhausted him;
it was that his chest had tightened with the fear of what lay ahead.
Head down, he left the barn, forcing his legs to carry him the short
distance to the house. He lifted his eyes and halted dead in his tracks.
There in front of him, standing in the exact same spot where he had
left her, was Ruth. She wore the same blue calico dress she had worn
on the day he ran away, and was holding her doll in the crook of her

right arm and their father's tintype in her tiny hand. Tom could not move for several minutes; he simply stood and stared. When at last he regained control of his limbs, he walked up to her. She smiled and motioned for him to bend down, as she had that morning not so very long ago. He did, and she whispered, "Home." The word warmed him, restoring strength to his legs and lifting the weight from his chest. With her other hand, she grasped Tom's and led him toward the back porch.

Tom opened the door. His mother sat at the kitchen table, sewing, her back to him. "Ruth," she said, "bring me that cloth on the stool by the door. I don't know why I set it there when I knew I'd need it."

Ruth didn't move to get the cloth. Instead, she pushed Tom toward the stool. He picked up the small swatch and stepped quietly to the table, laying it down with a gentle, "Here it is, mother."

Rebecca Scott dropped her sewing into her lap. She didn't turn around, but asked in a voice shaking with emotion, "Is that you, Thomas?"

"Yes, mother," Tom managed to say, his words barely audible.

Ruth tiptoed over to her mother and put a hand on her shoulder. Tom heard her say softly, "Home."

Rebecca rose from her seat, and in one motion turned, grabbed Tom, and pulled him into her arms. She sobbed on his shoulder. Tom cried too. Ruth hugged the both of them, smiling and saying over and over, "Home. Home. Home."

Repeatedly Tom mumbled through his tears, "I'm sorry," over and over again.

How many times Tom repeated those words over the next few days, he could not count. He did know that he meant them every time. He also told his mother that he loved her, something he had not told her for years. Now that he heard himself saying it, he could not understand why it had been so difficult. His crazy ideas of being too "grown up" and being a "man" had somehow gotten in the way. He found that he felt no less "grown up" saying it. As for being a "man," he now knew that he had a ways to go yet. He was very thankful that his mother had forgiven him. She had not said it in words, but her hugs, each time he got close enough for her to take him in her arms, showed him more than words ever could have.

Sitting under the old tree along the creek, Jake on his one side and Peter on the other, Tom told his friends what had happened after his mother had finished hugging him on his first day back home. "She wanted to know why I ran away."

"That's what my ma wanted to know too," admitted Peter. "What did you tell her?"

"The truth. That I wanted to be with Pa and be a drummer. That I thought he was all alone and needed me."

"Did she believe you?"

"Yes . . . I think. It was the truth, and I guess she understood. She hugged me after, and said I was very brave but very foolish. Then we cried some more and . . ."

"I never thought I'd ever hear you say that you cried, Tom."

"Me neither, but I did, and I've cried almost every day since, every time she hugs me."

"You tell her about your pa?" asked Jake.

"That was what she wanted to know next. She was happy that he was doing well but shocked when I told her he had a beard and was thin. She misses him real bad."

"Did you tell her about all that happened to us and to you?"

"Not everythin'."

"Why not?"

163

"'Cause some of it was too scary. If she knew what I had gotten into . . ."

"You're goin' to tell us, ain't you?"

"If I do, you got to promise never to tell nobody. If you do I'll . . . I'll thrash you."

All three boys burst out laughing, and then Tom told his tale. As he had with his mother, he did not tell everything, omitting parts of what had happened since he had returned home. These had to do with his relationship with his mother. That he wanted to keep to himself. He understood that his mother believed that he was still a boy and that the boy in him had caused him to run away. His having traveled alone for over a hundred miles all by himself didn't matter one bit. To her he was only a boy, not the man his father wanted him to be. His father had often allowed him to drive the wagon when they were out of sight of the farm. Tom thought his mother must know it, but still she would not give him the reins when she was with him. A half- acre of land had yet to be plowed when he arrived home, but when it came time to plow it, his mother walked behind the plow while he walked beside the horses. The barn roof needed repairing. Tom had been running around on that roof – the side not visible from the house – since he was ten, jumping off it into the hay wagon, but his mother hired someone to fix it instead of giving the job to her son. Tom wanted to talk to her about it, but feared to do so. He didn't want to spoil the new closeness he felt, so he kept silent and waited, hoping that somehow the day would come when she would see that he was growing up; had grown up so very much in so many ways, and wasn't a boy any longer.

Tom first heard the news that a great battle had been fought in Virginia when he went to Mr. Shannon's Variety Store on an errand for his mother. He listened intently to everything the men had to say as they talked about it outside the store. He remembered his father telling him that the army might move out soon, and it had, only to be defeated once again. Tom felt sick to his stomach when he heard one man say that the army had suffered many, many casualties. One of the other men elbowed the man who had spoken. Tom heard him say quietly, "Don't say anything more. That boy's father is with the army."

Tom started for home. All kinds of thoughts ricocheted around inside his head. He would not allow them to form into questions. Questions wanted answers, and he might not like some of the answers his mind would come up with. By the time he reached for the latch on the kitchen door, he had made up his mind not to tell his mother anything. When he opened the door, he saw that she already knew. Johnny Myers's mother sat across the table from Rebecca Scott. The two looked pale, and Tom could see that they had been crying. Having heard the door open behind her, Tom's mother stood up, faced him, and said, "There's been a battle."

"Yes," Tom replied, "I heard about it in town. Did you hear anything about Pa?"

"It's too soon, but the army has suffered a great number of . . ."

"I know," interrupted Tom in an effort to save his mother from saying what she feared most.

Tom didn't want to, but he sat down at the table, saying nothing until after Mrs. Myers left. Then he tried to persuade his mother that his father would have taken care of himself because of her and him and Ruth. Even as he heard himself speak, he knew he didn't sound very convincing and decided not to say any more. Ruth joined them, and they sat quietly until his mother began to prepare supper.

Over the next several days the battle became the subject that neither Tom nor his mother talked about. Tom began to avoid her just so he wouldn't be tempted to talk to her about it. He even called a meeting of the Invincibles, the first of the new year just to get away from the house. On the day of the gathering, every one of the boys showed up eager to drill and shoot their slingshots, but even more eager to hear about Tom's adventures.

"You're goin' to tell us all about what you did after Jake and Peter left you," Billy Boyd pleaded. "Ain't you?"

"Did they tell you anythin'?" Tom asked, throwing a nasty look at Jake and Peter.

"All they told us was what happened on the way to the river. I liked the parts about you hiding in the mill and in the barn. I would've been too scared to do that."

"They didn't tell you anythin' about what happened after that?"

"You mean they know! You already told them! Ahh, Tom, now you got to tell us!"

"My pa says he heard about a fight on a canal boat," declared Ben Rankin, "and that you were in it. He say's you were a real hero. Was it really you?"

"How did he hear about that?" Looking at Jake and Peter, Tom added, "Did you . . .?"

"Honest, Tom," insisted Jake. "We didn't tell anybody what you told us."

Tom didn't know whether to believe him or Peter, who shook his head vigorously. To the rest of the Invincibles he said, "I don't know if I should tell you. You might not be able to keep it a secret. I don't want my ma to find out. If she did, I'd really catch it."

"You just order us not to tell," Ben suggested. "If it's an order we got to obey it."

Every Invincible nodded or grunted in agreement. In the end Tom gave the order and repeated his adventures to the boys. The boys sat mesmerized. When Tom demonstrated how he used his slingshot against the canal boat raiders, the Invincibles took out their slingshots and joined thwacking nearby trees that took the place of the raiders. After Tom finished, the Invincibles gave him three cheers, lifted him on their shoulders and carried him around the tree several times until they all fell in a heap. Once they caught their breaths, Billy spoke up, "I think we should promote Tom to major."

"And Jake to captain," yelled Ben.

"And Peter to lieutenant," added Johnny Myers.

A quick show of hands and a cheer followed. By the time he walked home, Tom's head had swelled several sizes. He wondered if his mother would notice.

The letter came on May 12. Tom's mother had driven Tom and Ruth into Mercersburg, having a number of items to purchase that Tom could not have carried home by himself. He had wanted to take the wagon alone and tried to convince his mother to allow him to, but she refused and then stared him down when he started to protest. He couldn't bring himself to argue with her, not after what he had put her through. In town she sent him to the post office while she and Ruth went shopping. When the postmaster handed him the letter, Tom jumped for joy. He recognized his father's handwriting and knew without opening the letter that his father had escaped the battle.

"He still may have been wounded," said Rebecca Scott, as she took the letter from Tom's hand, "and is lying in some hospital slowly . . ." Tom put his arms around her. He had not thought of that possibility, and it struck him like a kick from a mule. Tom looked at Ruth. There was a calm expression on her face. She smiled as she held up their father's tintype and said, "Pa."

Rebecca Scott, determined to spare her children any bad news, sent them from the kitchen as she sat down to read her husband's letter.

Dearest Rebecca,

Jeremiah and I have passed through the horrors of the recent battle and by the blessings of God have emerged unscathed. Our regiment was spared the terrible conflict that raged near a place called Chancellorsville. We fought along the Rappahannock River at United States Ford. The brigade was to cross the river there. Our regiment was the only one to really do any fighting. I will not describe what it is like to be in a battle. It would only cause you to worry about us all the more.

I wanted to write to you before this, but the movement of our army prevented me. Please do not be too hard on Thomas. Our son was trying to help me by coming here. He thought that I was alone and needed him. In truth, I miss you all so deeply that I ache from it, but it is what I must bear. To end this war as quickly as possible is my greatest desire, so that I can come home to all of you. I had hoped that a victory would bring this horrible conflict to a close. Now that we have suffered yet another defeat, I am at a loss to know how long it will take or even if we can succeed.

Jeremiah sends his love. He is well. We have become hard men who endure far more than we ever could have believed. Only the thought of you waiting for me at home provides the strength I need to face each new day.

I must close this letter as the fire is dying and taps will soon sound. Embrace Tom and Ruth for me and close your eyes, as I do every night, and think of us a family once again.

Your loving husband,

Jonathan

As he waited with Ruth on the porch, Tom listened intently for any sound coming from the kitchen. When he heard none, he breathed a sigh of relief. The silence told him that his father was well and so was Uncle Jeremiah. His mother called him and Ruth back into the house and told them a little of what their father had written. Tom, thinking of Ruth, did not ask any questions. A few days later while his mother hung up wash to dry, he sneaked into his mother's room and read the letter for himself. He nearly jumped out of his skin when the creak of a floorboard scared him. Whirling around, expecting his mother to be glaring at him, he saw Ruth. She made a pouting face, said, "Bad Tom," and went back down the stairs. He knew she wouldn't tell on him, but her catching him made him feel guilty for the rest of the day.

Johnny Myers's mother also waited for a letter, but it never came. Her husband had fought at Chancellorsville with the One Hundred and Twenty-sixth Pennsylvania. The regiment's Company C contained men from Mercersburg, and while his name did not appear on the casualty lists, she was haunted by the fact that no one seemed to know anything. Finally on May 15, Major Robert J. Brownson of the regiment came home to Mercersburg and announced that Company C was in Harrisburg and would be mustered out soon. Later that day,

Johnny Myers came whooping and hollering to the old tree where the Invincibles were meeting again. "My pa's coming home! My pa's coming home!" he kept yelling. It took several minutes for Tom and Jake to calm him down enough to talk clearly. "He's coming home. My ma said his time in the army is over. He's coming home with a lot of the men from town."

"When?" asked Tom, hoping that his own father would be with them. "Is the war over?"

"I don't know. I don't think it is, but my ma said that my pa's company has served out its time, and he is coming home to stay."

Tom raced across the field, not caring if he trampled the young corn that had emerged from the ground over the past several weeks. He burst into the kitchen nearly knocking his mother over. "Johnny Myers said his father is comin' home. He's not in the army any more. Is Pa comin' home too?"

At the shock of the news, Rebecca staggered back into the table and steadied herself against it. "Ruth! Ruth!" she called. "We'll go over to Mrs. Myers and see. If the war is over, then . . ."

The town of Mercersburg celebrated the homecoming of many of its sons on the evening of May 23. The war was not over. Jonathan Scott would not be coming home. Many of the men of Mercersburg's Company C of the One Hundred and Twenty-sixth Pennsylvania had completed their time of service. Tom's father was in a different regiment, and his time of service was not up. Even so, Tom's mother insisted that they join in the celebration to welcome the men back. As Tom stood with many of Mercersburg's citizens in the square in front of Col. Murphy's hotel and watched the company march down the street, he couldn't take his eyes off his mother. She smiled and cheered, as did the rest of the crowd, but there was sadness in her eyes. He moved close to her, brushing up against her side. Without looking, she put her arm around him and drew him to her. Ruth stood next to him, holding his hand.

The "Welcome Home" ceremonies included a large choir, made up of the choirs of several churches, that sang two beautiful songs. Several prominent men of the town, including Dr. Creigh, spoke. Tom listened carefully to every word. Most times he didn't pay much attention in church, but something made him want to hear what was said about the men and what they had endured. In some way the words brought his father closer, knowing that he was going through some of the same hardships these men had passed through. A voice inside him kept repeating that if these men had come home after passing through so much, so would his father.

After the ceremonies ended, the company broke up and the men reunited with their families. Tom, his mother, and Ruth started homeward. Through the thinning crowd Tom saw Johnny Myers and his mother hugging Johnny's father. All three were crying and laughing at the same time. For a moment Tom shared their joy, but a glance at his mother, her cheeks wet with silent tears, drove it from him. The sadness that took its place was even greater than it had been before. It lasted through a sleepless night and into the next day. At breakfast he asked, "Are you happy for Mrs. Myers?"

His mother looked up from her plate and answered, "Yes, Thomas. Oh, yes. I am very happy for her. She has been through so much for so long."

"How can you be happy and sad at the same time? I know you're sad because Pa isn't home."

"Thomas, I want your father to come home more than anything in the world. The happiness I feel for Mrs. Myers is a small part of the happiness I will feel when your father returns to us. When he does, I know I will feel the same way as Mrs. Myers, and that gives me strength to go on. It gives me hope."

Ruth held up the tintype, said, "Pa!" and smiled.

"Yes, dearest. Your pa will come home to us and we will all be a family again, just like the Myerses."

At the next meeting of the Invincibles Johnny and two of the other boys, whose fathers had returned with Company C, were missing. Tom started the drilling, his voice tinged with anger. As he barked out the orders, he slowly began to realize that he was not so much angry with Johnny and the others as he was jealous of them. They had what he wanted and couldn't have. He turned the drilling over to Jake, who gave him a confused look, and stood by the tree until the time came for target practice. Tom's mind refused to concentrate and he lost the accuracy contest for the first time to Ben. He shrugged it off. Losing didn't matter to him as much as it had before. At one time he would have made all kinds of excuses or just whupped Ben. Now he congratulated him, dismissed the company, and started home. Jake caught up with him.

"What's wrong with you?"

"What do you mean?"

"You shot terrible."

"Ben just beat me, that's all."

"That ain't all. I know you. You don't like losin' at anythin'."

"I was mad 'cause Johnny and the other boys weren't here. Awww, I wasn't mad. I was . . ."

"Yeah, I guess it was hard to see Johnny's pa come home when yours . . ."

"Listen, Jake. Maybe you better take over the Invincibles for a while. I think I should spend more time at home with my ma. She needs me."

"That's what you said when you ran away to your pa."

Tom didn't reply. He knew that what Jake said was right. He had changed. He felt – responsible for his mother, for her happiness, for her care. Whatever he could do to help her get through this time, he would. He'd be a boy or a man, whatever she needed him to be.

May became June, and another letter arrived.

Dearest Rebecca,

I seat myself down next to a roaring fire to write and tell you that I am in good health and have even gained a little weight. Jeremiah is well too and sends his love. The army is recovering and growing stronger every day. We have heard nothing of what is to come, though there are rumors aplenty. General Hooker talks much less about whipping Bobby Lee since Bobby Lee whipped him. The army wants another fight, as we know we can win if we are well led. We are no longer sure that Hooker is the man to do it.

Your last three letters found their way to me at last. What joy I felt on opening and reading them. I read them several times and even had Jeremiah read them aloud to me. I am happy that you and Thomas are closer now. You must entrust him with those things that he can do. He is nearly a man and can do much to help you.

Are the crops doing well? Did you get them planted in time? Did you have to hire someone to help you? I hope that you did not try to do all the planting yourself.

I heard from a member of the One Hundred and

Twenty-sixth that Company C was mustered out and went home. I am happy for the men and their families and jealous too, for I long to see all of you.

Please kiss Tom – even if he doesn't like it – and Ruth for me, and hug them too. Tell them I miss them terribly. My thoughts are always about you.

Your loving husband,

Jonathan

Tom didn't have to sneak into his mother's room to read the letter, as she read it after dinner the day she received it. He asked her to read it again and watched very carefully when she read the part about how she should let him help her more because he was nearly a man. He could not detect any change in her appearance, and the days after did not show any change in the way she treated him.

The war returned suddenly to Mercersburg. Tom first learned of it when Johnny Myers's father rode up the lane and into the barnyard. Tom's mother was feeding the chickens, and Mr. Myers spoke to her without dismounting, "Mrs. Scott."

"Yes, George? It's good to see you again."

"I bear grave news. A portion of the Confederate army has crossed the Potomac near Clear Spring and is headed for us. It is not known whether this is an invasion or simply a raid such as the town suffered last October, but you must take all precautions. Hide your valuables, food, and horses."

"Won't our army stop them?"

"By all appearances, our army is still south of the river. They will give us no aid. The Rebels could be here in a few days."

"Thank you, George. You take care of your family. We'll be fine.

I'll do what Jonathan did the last time the Rebels came."

"Very well, but if you need anything, send Tom for me."

Watching Mr. Myers ride away, Tom thought about the last time the infernal Confederate Rebels came to town. Even his fond memories of General Stuart could not hide the fact that if the Rebels did come again, his family might not be as fortunate as they had been. They had lost nothing then. This time they could lose everything.

"Mother," he asked as he walked up to her, "should I hide the horses where Pa did the last time?"

At first his mother didn't speak but stood staring after Mr. Myers. Tom heard her mutter to herself, "If only I had not given Jonathan back his promise. He'd be here to . . ."

"Mother, it'll be alright. I'll take the horses and . . ."

"Yes, Thomas, take them to the hiding place. Ruth and I will start gathering things in the house. We'll have to hide some things out in the woods."

"What about the meat in the smokehouse?"

"Yes, we'll have to hide most of that too. I'll get a barrel. We can bury it out in the woods as well."

By late the next day Mercersburg had made what preparations it could to receive unwelcomed guests. Stores had closed. The merchants had packed up most of their wares and sent them away. Tom hid the horses and the family's valuables, such as they were, in the little gully where his father had concealed the horses after Ruth's warning. On his way back to the house, Tom wondered about his sister. She had not said a thing about the coming invasion. *Maybe*, he thought, *the Rebels will miss Mercersburg this time.*

The next day the Invincibles gathered to talk about what they should do if the infernal Confederate Rebels did come again. Tom tried to talk them out of doing anything, but they kept saying that

175

he had beaten the river raiders with his slingshot, so they could send these Rebels back over the river too. He tried to explain, but got nowhere. He even reminded them of their paroles that they had given to General Stuart. In the end he ordered them not to fight, but he saw that it was one order that some of them would not obey.

After two more days, Tom began to think that his father's army must have stopped the Rebels. He became so sure of it that he decided to ask to his mother about bringing the horses and other things back from where they had been hidden. As he approached the house from the barn he saw Ruth standing on the porch, pointing off into the distance. He knelt beside her and whispered, "Horses?"

She nodded.

CHAPTER 11

Gettysburg

T om saw a cloud of dust, billowing above the trees to the west in the direction of Cove Mountain. He picked up Ruth, carried her inside, and told his mother, "There's dust rising west of town. I think the Rebels are coming."

"It could be our army, come to protect us."

"Mr. Myers said that our army was still south of the river."

"But they could have caught the Rebels and beaten them and are now . . . No. Of course you're right, Thomas. We'll just stay here in the house. Perhaps they will pass by us."

Tom learned later that the Rebels had been a force of cavalry under a man named Ferguson. His men, driving dozens of horses along with them and laden with plunder, passed through Mercersburg without causing too much damage, except for some horses taken from a few local farmers. The town breathed a sigh of relief, knowing that it could have been far worse. Tom was very thankful that Rebels came and went so quickly. Those members of the Invincibles that wanted to fight them had no time to react. Tom later found out that most of the boys had run afoul of their mothers, who had confiscated their slingshots and ammunition and, in the case of three of them, locked them in their rooms. Only Ben Rankin managed to get a shot at the enemy.

Tom knew that Ben was both smart and sneaky. According to what Ben told the Invincibles weeks later, he had tied his slingshot to one leg and his ammunition bag to the other and sat quietly while his mother searched his room, high and low. She finally gave up but took the precaution of locking Ben in his room, thinking he could not possibly get into any mischief there. Ben had other plans. As the Rebels trotted down the street in front of his house, he crawled out a window onto a nearby tree limb and weaved his way through the branches until he overlooked the street. Patiently he waited until the last set of four mounted men rode by and then fired a single shot, hitting the rump of one of the men's horses. The horse bolted ahead, scattering men and horses in several directions and unseating not a few very angry Rebel riders. Ben nearly fell out of the tree laughing and just managed to get back into his room before his mother, hearing the ruckus outside and suspecting her son had something to do with it, unlocked the door and entered. She found Ben, lying on his bed, reading. He smiled, and she retreated in defeat. She found the slingshot that night when Ben went to bed. And so the last shot of the Invincibles for the rest of the war was fired.

Five days later, the Rebel invasion came to Mercersburg with a vengeance. An entire brigade of infantry, over a hundred cavalry, and six pieces of artillery, about 2,000 men in all, marched into town, and this was only the beginning. For the next week Rebels came and went. Each new group wrought new havoc on the citizens. Food, horses, cattle, sheep, and store goods, the last again paid for with worthless Confederate money, disappeared from homes, farms, and store shelves. Through it all, Tom managed to save the horses and the wagon. He had not thought about the wagon until he heard from Jake that the Rebels were taking wagons to

178

haul off the other things they had plundered. Neither Tom nor the crazed rooster could save the chickens this time, however, and when General Imboden came through town and demanded 5,000 pounds of bacon, 20 barrels of flour, and other foodstuffs on the threat of occupying the houses, the Scotts suffered along with their neighbors. They gave up much of their smoked meat, which Tom dug up and took out of the barrel where they had hidden it, although they, like others, kept back a little for the future when the Rebels would be gone, or so everyone hoped.

Along with the Rebels came rumors of what was happening beyond the confines of Mercersburg and Franklin County. The vague reports that a great battle would be fought somewhere in the state aroused in Tom's mother more fear and worry than the loss of the chickens or the meat. Tom understood why. His father and Uncle Jeremiah very probably would be in any battle to be fought. Not knowing what was happening to them ate away at Rebecca Scott. Until she knew, knew for certain, that her husband and brother were safe, she would have no peace. Tom did all he could to comfort her, but instead of being able to relieve her of her fear, he came to share it. *If only I had stayed with Pa,* he told himself.

July came with its heat and humidity. The Rebels had gone, although everyone believed they would return. Tom went about his morning chores, including checking on the horses in the gully down by Johnston Run. Then he worked in the barn until near noon when his mother called to him from the back porch.

"Thomas! Thomas! I can't find Ruth. Is she out there with you?"

"No, I haven't seen her since breakfast."

"Will you look for her? I want her to try on this new dress I'm

179

making for her."

Tom grumbled to himself, knowing that his sister was undoubtedly somewhere around the barn or house, hiding, as she often did, off in a world of her own. When she was like that she would not answer or come when you called her. He searched the barn first and finding nothing, ran into the house. Rushing upstairs, he looked in places he knew Ruth liked to crawl into and hide, but she was in none of them. As he came downstairs, greatly puzzled and a little angry, he heard a faint sound from outside the front door. Opening it, he found Ruth sitting on a porch step. That was not unusual, but what she was doing, was. She was crying. Tom had never seen his sister cry, and it scared him.

"Mother!" Tom yelled. "Mother, come quick! Somethin's wrong with Ruth!"

Tom stepped out onto the porch and stood behind his sister. His mother joined him. Together they began to bend over Ruth when unexpectedly she turned around. Tears streamed down her face as she held up her father's tintype. "Pa," she sobbed.

Tom felt his mother collapse against him. He managed to catch her before she fell and helped her to sit down on a bench that was built into the porch. Ruth, still crying, climbed up to her and buried her head in her mother's lap. "Ma! Ma!" Tom cried, not knowing exactly what had happened or what to do. He ran to the kitchen for water. By the time he returned, his mother was conscious and held Ruth in her arms.

"What is it, Ma? Why is Ruth cryin'? She never cries!"

"I've always tried to ignore Ruth's strangeness, but your pa trusted it. He would say she was blessed with it for a reason. If this is the reason, it can't be a blessing."

"I don't understand. What's wrong?"

"Thomas, something has happened to your father."

Tom felt his own knees buckle. He slid down the wall and buried his face in his arms. It *couldn't be true* - he told himself over and over. He refused to believe it. His pa had told him that he and Uncle Jeremiah would take care of each other. Nothing could have happened to him. Tom raised his head and looked at Ruth. She had known he was going to run away. She had been waiting for him when he returned. She knew the Rebels were coming before anyone else. How? How did she know these things? No. It didn't matter how she knew them. It only mattered that she did – and she had never been wrong. The pain of that thought washed over him, soaking the truth of what his sister had said into him. Something **had** happened to his father. Suddenly, the meaning of his father's words came to him more strongly than ever before, "Remember, you must take care of your mother and Ruth."

Ruth cried herself to sleep in her mother's lap. Rebecca sat stroking her daughter's hair and gazing out across the fields, seeing nothing. Tom, crumpled at her feet, had no strength to move or talk. The sun arced through the heavens until it perched on Cove Mountain to the west. Nothing stirred. Not even the birds sang. The quiet both calmed and frightened Tom. He could remain there through the night, he thought, but his father's words struck him anew. He must take care of his mother and sister. Rising stiffly to his feet, he gently touched his mother's arm. She looked at him and understood.

News of a battle reached Mercersburg over the next few days. Much of what was told proved false. Tom, torn between wanting to know and not wanting to know, kept much of it from his mother,

181

who stayed close to the farm. On July 5, a body of Union cavalry stopped in town. The people did their best to make the soldiers feel welcome, providing what refreshments they could from the meager supplies left to them by the Rebels. Tom had come into town at his mother's urging to pick up any mail, hoping to hear something from his father or Uncle Jeremiah. Tom realized that it was too soon after the battle, if one had really taken place, but did as his mother wished. He listened intently to the soldiers and learned that a battle had indeed been fought at Gettysburg. The Rebels had been defeated and were retreating. A few people who had been fleeing from the Rebel army, which swarmed the countryside looking for all sorts of supplies and plunder, talked to the officer in charge of the soldiers. They told him about a vast wagon train passing through Chambersburg and Greencastle and moving toward Williamsport. The blue cavalry rode off toward Greencastle. Tom hurried home.

The next day, July 6, Constable Wolfe rode up the lane. Tom saw him coming and ran for the house, afraid of the news he might bear. The knock on the front door echoed through a house quiet with fear. Tom walked with his mother to the door. She opened it. "I'm very sorry to bother you, Mrs. Scott," Mr. Wolfe began. Tom's eyes never left his mother's face. "I've come to ask if you will come to town and assist the other women of the church. A portion of the enemy's wagon train has been captured. Many of the wagons were filled with wounded. The more serious cases are being placed in the seminary and some of the churches. We are in need of nurses to care for the injured men. I understand that this is asking a great deal of you, being that your husband has fought these people, but . . ."

"Say no more Constable Wolfe. I will pack up some linen and

what supplies I have that might be of help and come immediately."

"Thank you, Mrs. Scott. I shall tell them at the seminary that you are coming. God bless you."

The door closed. Tom watched his mother as she stood quietly for a few minutes. Unable to contain himself he asked, 'Why are you going to help those Rebels. If Pa is hurt or . . . One of them might've . . ."

"Thomas. I'm going because if your father has been hurt, I would hope that someone would take care of him even though he was an enemy. Will you help me get the things together? Then I must go and leave you here with Ruth."

"I want to go with you."

"I know, but you must stay here and take care of your sister."

As Tom stood and watched his mother drive away in the wagon, he fought to push the image of the wounded soldiers lying in the seminary out of his mind. They all had his father's face. He had to do something to keep from thinking about them. Taking Ruth by the hand, he ran to the barn and began to do his chores. Ruth sat to one side, holding her doll and the tintype. Every few minutes she sniffed and wiped her eyes with her little apron. Finally Tom sat with her, his arm around her shoulders.

The next few days passed in a blur. Tom watched as his mother got up before dawn, made breakfast, gathered her few things, and drove off to the seminary. She returned well after dark, exhausted, her clothes sometimes blood stained. Tom, much better at eating than cooking, did his best to have a little meal prepared for her. Ruth had not said a word for days, so Tom tried to get his mother to talk, but she said very little. No news came about his father or Uncle Jeremiah.

183

Jake came to visit about four days after the wounded soldiers arrived. "Where've you been?" he asked, a tinge of concern in his words.

"My ma's been nursin' the wounded soldiers in the seminary, so I got to stay home and watch Ruth."

"My ma's been at one of the churches. I got my sister watchin' me like a hawk. She tries to order me around. If I don't do it, she'll tell my ma. I'm still in trouble for runnin' away, so I do what she says 'cause I don't want my ma to be mad at me."

"You see any of the soldiers?"

"No, my ma said for me to stay away."

"They must be hurt real bad for them to be left here and not go back with their army."

"Yeah. I heard my ma tell Johnny's ma that some have died from their wounds and . . . I'm sorry, Tom. I forgot that your pa . . ."

"We ain't heard nothin', but Ruth started cryin' 'bout a week ago and held up Pa's tintype. I ain't never seen her cry before. Ma thinks somethin' happened to Pa."

"My ma says your sister knows things the rest of us don't. Does she?"

"All I know is that my pa always listened to her when she said anythin'. He saved our horses that way when General Stuart came last year."

"Did she say that somethin' happened to your pa?"

"No, it was like I told you. She just held up his picture and said, 'Pa', but she was cryin' when she did it. My ma fell over on me. I didn't know what to do."

"Well, I think I'll take my sister the way she is; bossy. If Ruth was my sister, I'd be scared most of the time."

"She does scare me sometimes, but she's my sister, and Pa told me to take care of her and my mother, and that's what I'm goin' to do."

Jake stayed for a couple of hours. The boys took turns shooting Tom's slingshot. Jake's mother had not given his back to him yet. He hoped she hadn't thrown it away. Tom showed him that he still had two pieces of rubber so even if she had he could make another one.

For another ten days, Tom's mother went to the seminary to help care for the wounded men. Bored as he was, having to stay around the farm, Tom never once complained. He woke each day with his father's words in his mind, and they were his last thought when he went to bed each night. Then late one afternoon near the end of the month, Mr. Myers came riding up the lane. Tom met him in front of the barn.

"I suspect that your mother is at the seminary, Tom," Mr. Myers said as he stepped down from his horse.

"Yes. She'll not be back 'til after dark."

"She has worked very hard. I know because my wife has been helping there too."

"Did somethin' happen?"

"No, no, as far as I know your mother is fine. What brings me here is this letter. The postmaster asked me to bring it. I know you have not heard from your father since the battle, so I . . ."

"Is it a letter from my pa?"

"I don't know, Tom. It was not my place to open it, and if I were you, I'd wait until your mother gets home before you open it. Promise me that you will."

Tom stared at the letter in Mr. Myers's hand. He wanted to tear it open right now and find out what it said, but he understood that Mr. Myers was right. "I promise to wait for my ma."

185

"Thank you, Tom. I hope and pray it is good news."

Holding the letter and watching Mr. Myers ride away, Tom regretted his promise almost immediately. He looked at the letter and saw that the envelope did not have his father's handwriting on it. It was Uncle Jeremiah's. Tom trembled, slipped one finger inside a little opening in the envelope, as he had often seen his mother do, and nearly tore it open. His promise to Mr. Myers popped into his head. Tom had been doing better with promises lately. At one time they had meant very little to him – just so many words. But his father had kept his promise, even though it caused him to be looked down on by half the town. Now, the promise he had made to his father, the one he had done everything to keep, stopped him. He slid his finger out of the envelope, walked into the house, and set the letter on the kitchen table. From there it haunted him for the remainder of the day.

When Rebecca Scott returned and sat down wearily at the table her eyes immediately fell on the envelope. She gasped as she looked at Tom. "I promised Mr. Myers, he brought it, that I wouldn't open it. I wanted to, Ma, but . . ."

"I'm not sure I want to open it, but I must. I must know."

Dearest Sister,

    With a heavy heart I take pen in hand to tell you that which I know will bring you great sorrow. Our army has fought a great battle here at Gettysburg. On the first day, our regiment fought hard but was driven back by overwhelming numbers of Rebels. During our retreat an enemy shell burst above us. I was struck in the leg by a piece of the shell and fell. Some of our men picked me up to carry me back with them. I looked for Jonathan. He was not among them. I asked them to stop and find him, but one said that he had been lying next to me. He had been struck by a piece of the same shell. To spare you greater grief, I shall not describe the wound he suffered, but the man believed that he was killed. We were forced to leave him behind with many others of our wounded and dead. I grieve with you, Rebecca. Jonathan was like a brother to me. You must be brave and temper your loss with the knowledge that he fell in a noble cause and gave himself to halt our enemy here on the soil of our beloved commonwealth.

I am slowly recovering. The doctors have been able to save my leg, though I am afraid it will not be of much use to me for a long time. You are my only family. I ask if you could come and take me home with you. I am sure I can persuade one of the doctors to permit me to go with you. There are so many wounded men here. One less will be a boon to the others. Our division hospital is near the White Church along the Baltimore Pike.

Your loving brother,
Jeremiah

Tom read the letter after his mother. She sat still and silent as he read. He wanted to shout that it was a lie; that none of it was true. Ruth stood next to him, looking over his shoulder at words she could not comprehend. Her sense had told her weeks ago that this had happened. She had cried for days. Now she held up the tintype, smiled, and said, "Pa." Tom pulled her to him, hugging her as he whispered, "Yes, Pa." He couldn't bring himself to tell her but then remembered that she had known that something had happened before he or their mother.

"So you're goin' to get your uncle?" Jake asked, not wanting to bring up the subject of Tom's father.

"Yeah, we're leavin' tomorrow," Tom replied. "Don't know how long it'll take. My ma says it depends on how much travelin' Uncle Jeremiah can stand."

"Where'll you stay?"

"Mr. Myers has relatives living outside Chambersburg. We'll stay with them tomorrow night and go on to Gettysburg the next day. Don't know what we'll do comin' home with Uncle Jeremiah."

"You takin' Ruth."

"I don't want to, but Ma says she needs Ruth to be with us. That we got to always do everythin' we can together from now on 'cause we're all the family we have."

"I think I know what she means. My ma said seein' my place empty at the table for those days I was gone made her cry, but she kept puttin' my plate there, like I was goin' to sit down any minute. She said that my not bein' there made the rest of the family come closer together."

"You still that way?"

"I guess. My sister and me don't fight as much."

"Ruth and me never fought. I'm tryin' to understand her more and; my ma too."

After a long silence, Jake finally said, "I'm sorry 'bout your pa."

Tom nodded, the words he wanted to say sticking in his throat.

The next morning, Tom clambered up onto the wagon seat. His mother handed Ruth to him. Sitting her next to him, he took up the reins and held the horses steady as his mother climbed on. For a second, Tom thought she was going to let him drive, but instead she looked at him and held out her hands. He started to say something but saw her eyes harden and her brow furrow. He handed over the reins without saying a word.

During the time he had run away, Tom had not taken the opportunity to really see the country he was traveling through. Except for his time on the *Decatur*, he had been too worried about being caught to notice much. Now, as the wagon ambled slowly along, he had the opportunity to see the land, trees, fields, and sky. Of course he had nothing else to do. He didn't want to think about where he was going and why. Not that he didn't care about or disliked his uncle; it was just that he could not think of Uncle Jeremiah without thinking about his father, and that was something he had been trying hard to avoid so he could stay strong for his mother.

Tom remembered little of the trip or the stay at Mr. Myers's relatives. One thing he did recall vividly long afterward was the condition of the road. Hundreds of wagons and thousands of men and horses had passed over it just weeks before. The effects of their passing still showed in the ruts and discarded equipment they had left behind. The farms along the way had paid an equally heavy price, more so than those around Mercersburg. With many of their crops destroyed, farmers struggled to find horses to harvest what still stood in the fields. Several of them offered to buy the Scotts' horses. The desperate look in their eyes frightened Ruth and caused Tom to worry if their horses might be stolen from them. He uttered a prayer of thanks when the town of Gettysburg came into view on the second day of their journey.

The fields around the town still showed signs of the titanic battle that had raged across them. A stench hung in the air that Tom had never smelled before. Ruth cuddled close to him, muttering, "Bad place," repeatedly. Tom agreed. Their mother wept as she drove into the outskirts of the town. All along the road her eyes darted back and forth from one side to the other, as if she were searching for something. Tom knew what it was. He also knew she would never find it. Blue-coated soldiers rode and walked everywhere, and yellow flags hung from many buildings and outside scores of tents. In front of one of the tents Rebecca Scott pulled her wagon to a stop and called out to a nearby soldier. "We are trying to find my brother. He was wounded. He wrote that he is near the White Church on the Baltimore Pike. Can you help us?"

"I'm sorry, ma'am. You'll have to see the Provost Marshal. His headquarters are down that way. Just ask anyone. They'll direct you."

After several attempts, one soldier finally knew the location of the Provost Marshal's headquarters, but better than that, he knew where the White Church was located and gave clear directions. While driving through Gettysburg, Tom could see the evidence of the battle everywhere. Finding the Baltimore Pike proved easy, and before long the White Church loomed ahead. All around it crowded a large number of tents. People, some in uniform, came and went from them. One man approached, and Tom's mother drew rein and stopped.

"Ma'am," the soldier said. "You shouldn't be here. This is a hospital and not a place for your children to see."

"I've come for my brother. He's Private Jeremiah Reynolds. He was with the Fifty-sixth Pennsylvania. He wrote to me and asked me to come for him. May I see him or talk to someone about seeing him?"

"You'll have to talk to the surgeon in charge. He's that man standing over there. He will help you if he can."

"Thank you."

Tom sat, holding Ruth on his lap, and stared after his mother as she walked over to a man with a short beard, wearing a white apron. They talked for a time, the man eventually pointing toward one of the tents. When his mother returned she said, "I think it best for you to stay here with Ruth and the wagon. I'll go and see if I can find Jeremiah. The doctor said he thought he was in that tent over there."

"But I want to go with you," Tom argued.

"Thomas, this is a hospital. The men here were seriously wounded. I don't want you or Ruth to see that."

"You said that we must always be together from now on and face everythin' together as a family 'cause all we have is each other."

His mother lowered her head. When she raised it again, Tom saw her eyes brimming with tears. "Yes, Thomas. You are right. I did say that, but there are times when I must protect you . . ."

"Pa told me to take care of you and Ruth. I promised him I would. I can't keep that promise if you won't let me."

Silent moments passed. Tom could feel his heart beating rapidly inside his chest. Finally, his mother answered, "Very well, but you must keep Ruth with you at all times. Don't let go of her."

"I won't, Ma."

The sunlight filtering through the canvas walls of the tent fell on two long rows of cots. The men that lay on them, those that were awake and could move, turned to look as Tom pushed aside the tent flap and entered, his mother on one side and Ruth on the other. From down near the end of the tent came a cry of, "Rebecca! Rebecca!"

"Jeremiah," called Tom's mother, and she hurried to him, with Tom and Ruth close behind.

"You've come. You've come. I wasn't sure you would or even if my letter reached you. Oh, Rebecca, I am so sorry. If I had been given the choice, I would have taken Jonathan's . . ."

"Don't say that. Never feel that way. What happened was supposed to be. He is in a better place now, away from all this strife. Now you must come back to the farm with me, get well, and we'll all work hard to . . . to . . ."

Tom reached out and hugged his mother as she slumped down on the edge of the cot. Jeremiah, wincing a little as he lifted himself up on his elbows, reached out one arm to touch her. For a time they huddled quietly until, "I'm sorry. I promised myself that I would be brave and here I am . . ."

"Sister dear, you should not make such promises. We all miss him, you most of all. You, all of us, must mourn him in order to go on."

"I know, but it has been so very hard. Thomas has been so strong and Ruth . . . Ruth. Where is Ruth?"

"She's right here behind . . .," Tom answered, but on turning around, he saw that Ruth was gone.

"Where is she?"

"I only let go of her hand for a minute to . . ."

"Find her. We must find her."

At that moment a man entered the tent and shouted, "There's a little girl in the next tent. Does she belong to someone here? She should not be wandering . . ."

"Yes, yes, she's my daughter. Come Thomas. We must go and get her."

Hurrying into the next tent, Tom saw his sister sitting on the edge of a cot about halfway down the row. He led his mother toward her. Ruth kept staring at the man lying on the cot. His head was half covered in bandages and he appeared to be sleeping. Ruth turned. She was smiling and, holding up the tintype that never seemed to be out of her hands, said, "Pa."

Both Tom and his mother stopped a few steps from the cot. They looked first at Ruth, then the tintype, and finally at the man lying on the cot. Again, Ruth said, "Pa."

"Oh Ruth," her mother answered as she stared at the man, "That's not your fath . . ."

Tom stared too. The longer he looked the more he recognized the face of the man, although he could see only half of it. "Someone," his mother called out. "Someone please help us."

A doctor approached, "What is it? You should not be disturbing this man. He has been unconscious for a long time. He only awoke two days ago. Please, I must ask you to leave."

"Who is he?"

"We don't know. He was in a Confederate hospital until after the battle and then was brought here. He had nothing on his person to identify him. Do you know him?"

"Pa," Ruth cried again.

The man opened his eyes and mumbled, "Ruth, my dear Ruth. Where are your mother and Thomas?"

Tom sat on the wagon seat, again holding the reins to keep the horses still. Two hospital stewards placed Uncle Jeremiah on the back of the wagon next to Tom's father. The doctors had decided that both men had recovered sufficiently to be moved. Jonathan Scott's wound had been nearly healed. It was his mind that had not. Being with his family for the past few days had changed all

193

that. Ruth squeezed between her uncle and her father. She no longer held the tintype. That was in Tom's pocket. Looking back over his shoulder, Tom saw Ruth, her face glowing as she went back and forth saying, "Pa! Uncle! Pa! Uncle!"

Tom's mother walked from the tent where she had been talking to one of the doctors. She came up to the back of the wagon and started to climb on. Ruth looked at her and said, "Home."

Rebecca Scott lifted her eyes and looked at her son, "Yes. Home. Take us home, Thomas. Take us home."

HISTORY OR FICTION?

A book such as *Journey to Gettysburg* is a mixture of historical
and fictional people, places, and events. For the writer, the
history and the fiction are intertwined, but nevertheless clearly
distinguishable one from the other. At least, they should be. However,
for the reader who may not be as knowledgeable about the history
part of the book, a problem can arise in knowing who or what was
real and who or what was not. I hope to help remove some of this
confusion, if it exists, by explaining about the story and how it was
constructed by mixing history with fiction.

The event that changed everything for the fictional family of
Jonathan, Rebecca, Thomas, and Ruth Scott actually happened.
Maj. Gen. James Ewell Brown Stuart, more commonly known
as "Jeb" Stuart, did make a raid, the Chambersburg Raid, into
Pennsylvania in early October 1862, and he did stop in Mercersburg,
Pennsylvania. His "visit" became the perfect starting point for the
story because of the impact it had on the town. All the places in
Mercersburg mentioned in the book really did exist, and most still
do, although the town has grown larger than it was in Civil War
times. The buildings that housed the hotel and the stores are still
standing, as is the Steiger home where Stuart enjoyed a meal. The
Scott's farm and home were fictional. Johnston Run still winds
its way through part of the town. All of the town's citizens that
were taken prisoner in the story, except for the boys, were really
taken prisoner by General Stuart. All of the Invincibles and their
families were fictional characters. Constable Wolfe was really the
town's constable; Dr. Creigh was a minister; and James Bennett
really did serve in the War of 1812.

The towns and places mentioned in the story did exist at that time. Most can be visited today, including Four Locks on the Chesapeake and Ohio Canal. You can even ride on a canal boat, though you will not find Captain Mulligan's boat, *The Decatur*, anywhere around. Both the boat and the good captain were fictional. Because so many of the places north of the Potomac River still exist, it is possible to follow Tom's journey from the beginning to near Washington, although the majority of the several days' journey on the canal would have to be done by car today. Once you cross the river, retracing Tom's journey becomes more difficult. Washington and the surrounding communities have grown so large that it would be impossible to follow the sutler, Captain George Winslow, and Tom's route to Tom's father, until near the Occoquan River. After that, the back roads and woodland paths that the Gray Ghost traveled have either disappeared or long been forgotten. If you noticed in that part of the book, I did not tell exactly on what back roads and paths Captain Mosby took Tom. That's because I do not know, and nobody living today could know. It was a fictional journey after all. For this part you just have to close your eyes and imagine what it was like to be led through narrow roads and along winding forest tracks.

As for the Gray Ghost, Captain John Singleton Mosby; he really did exist, and he really was a big problem for the Union forces in that and other areas of Virginia. He appeared and disappeared like a ghost, and because he wore a gray uniform, he earned the nickname, "The Gray Ghost." The two men who helped Tom reach his father through the picket line were fictional characters.

Of course, the invasion of the north in June/July 1863 that resulted in the battle of Gettysburg, did happen. The Confederate troops that were mentioned in the story as having passed through

Mercersburg actually did, along with others I didn't mention. The seminary and many other buildings were used as hospitals for the Confederate wounded, so I could have Rebecca Scott help to care for them in the story; though, being fictional, she really didn't.

One part of the story required some interesting research. When I began to write, I was unsure about how Tom and his Invincibles would meet General Stuart. When I finally decided that they would be taken as prisoners to the general, I had to invent a reason. The best one I could think of was to have the Invincibles "defend" Mercersburg against the "infernal Confederate Rebels." That gave me one huge problem. What would the Invincibles use to defend their town? I wanted them to be able to "fight" but not really hurt anyone. The idea of using slingshots came to mind. But did slingshots exist back in 1863?

The slingshot is different from a bow that shoots arrows. A bow gets its power from the wood, not the string. The wood bends when you pull back on the string that connects the two ends of the bow. When you let the string go, the wood snaps back into its original shape, giving the arrow power to fly through the air to its target. Bowstrings have been made of different materials throughout the past. However, if you make a slingshot out of a piece of bowstring and a "Y" shaped piece of wood, you will not get any power from it. Why? Because the wood doesn't bend. In a slingshot the power comes from the "string" not the wood. To have a slingshot you must have a "string" that stretches and snaps back into its former shape in order to shoot the pebble. And what is slingshot "string" made from? Vulcanized rubber. That means I could not use a slingshot as a weapon for the Invincibles unless vulcanized rubber had been invented before 1862. That is what my research had to uncover. A man named Charles Goodyear

197

discovered the vulcanization process in 1839, and by 1860, the slingshot had been invented. This meant I could use the slingshot as a weapon for the Invincibles.

I need to mention one final historical fact, although it shows up nowhere in the story. James Buchanan, the fifteenth president of the United States, was born at Cove Gap in Franklin County in 1791, but six years later his family moved into Mercersburg. Amazingly, he was the president before Abraham Lincoln, who was president during the Civil War. President Buchanan was in office when the Southern states seceded and formed the Confederate States of America, and when the war began at Fort Sumter. He is the only president from Pennsylvania. I doubt that very many, if any, of Stuart's troopers knew this the day they rode though Mercersburg.

Mixing history and fiction can be very exciting and can make a good story. It is important to know the historical period you are writing about. Then you can wind your fictional plot and characters around the real people, places, and events. I hope I have done this successfully, and that you have enjoyed *Journey to Gettysburg*.

Robert J. Trout

ABOUT THE AUTHOR

A teacher and prominent historian for over forty years, Robert J. Trout has dedicated his life to illuminating the history of the Civil War. He is considered one of the leading experts on Southern cavalry.

For fourteen years he portrayed Major General J.E.B. Stuart in a living history group, which led to the publication of his first book *They Followed the Plume: The Story of J. E. B. Stuart and His Staff.*

He has authored eleven other books, including the acclaimed historical novel, *The Story of Red Eye: The Miracle Horse of Gettysburg. Journey to Gettysburg: One Family's Civil War* is his third work of fiction.

Made in the USA
Charleston, SC
11 July 2013